BAD DAY IN BABYLON

After seven years of marriage to Steve Bannister, Linda discovers that she really doesn't know her husband at all. Thinking she's comfortably settled, with a suitable lifestyle in a good town, she now must face moving on — at any time. It would be sudden — in the middle of the night, or during a meal, such is the threat of danger. Steve's past is catching up with him . . . the only way it can be stopped is with a smoking gun.

CLAYTON NASH

BAD DAY IN BABYLON

Complete and Unabridged

LINFORD
Leicester

First published in Great Britain in 2009 by
Robert Hale Limited
London

First Linford Edition
published 2011
by arrangement with
Robert Hale Limited
London

British Library CIP Data

Nash, Clayton.
   Bad day in Babylon. - -
   (Linford western library)
   1. Western stories.
   2. Large type books.
   I. Title II. Series
   823.9'2–dc22

   ISBN 978–1–44480–590–1

Published by
F. A. Thorpe (Publishing)
Anstey, Leicestershire

Set by Words & Graphics Ltd.
Anstey, Leicestershire
Printed and bound in Great Britain by
T. J. International Ltd., Padstow, Cornwall

This book is printed on acid-free paper

1

Snake Man

He always blamed the rattlesnake for his troubles.

For years afterwards he went out of his way to chase down and kill every rattler he saw on his drifting around the frontier. After a while he realized how stupid and futile this was, but, by then, he had earned the nickname of *Snake*.

It appealed to him for a time until he came to his senses and got on with his life instead of trying to wipe out the rattlesnake population.

But he would never forget that first rattler that had sparked his vengeance.

It was a diamondback, eight feet long and as thick as a man's wrist. Never touched him, but it killed his horse and set him afoot in wild country. He had

1

been drifting south for no good reason and had figured to cut through the edge of the Solitario Flats, a desert-like area fringed with mesquite and scrub, but which would save him several miles on his journey to San Lividio.

After he killed the lousy son-of-a-bitchin' rattler, he tried to catch his horse when it began to froth at the mouth, but, driven mad by the venom, it ran out into the alkali. A brief chase on foot, throat parched, eyes stinging, soon convinced him he would never catch it. And all he owned in the world was on that jughead's back.

The only thing to do was to seek what shade he could in the scrub and keep heading south: eventually, he would come across a trail that would lead him to San Lividio.

But he would be mighty thirsty by then.

No use thinking about it: get on with it.

★ ★ ★

An hour later, he was a wreck: a cowboy was made to ride, not travel afoot. Sure not in this lousy, waterless scrub. He had tried sucking small round pebbles and, to his alarm, had swallowed one, hawking and coughing until he was sure he must choke. But, though it produced a pain under the arch of his ribs, it didn't seem to do much harm.

Recovering from the shock, he sat down in the sparse shade of a tree, letting his heartbeat settle, getting his ragged breathing back into some kind of normal rhythm again.

Gradually, the roaring in his head subsided and he leaned back, closed his eyes — and realized he could hear voices. At first, he figured it was an illusion brought on by his exertions, but then he began to make out words.

' . . . *Think I dunno who it had to be told them lawmen where the getaway mounts were?*'

'*It weren't me, Mr Cordell, I swear!*'

The second voice was trembling with terror.

'It was you — no one else had the chance! You cost me the best part of twenty thousand bucks, you treacherous bastard. Not to mention four men shot down by the Border Patrol!'

The other man was screaming his innocence by now, sobbing, pleading for his life.

From where he had been sheltering from the sun, the snake-killer couldn't see the men, but he moved forward stealthily, parting the coarse, bleached brush — and there they were.

Four men in a small clearing not twenty yards away. One was down on his knees, hands clasped as he pleaded for his life. A big man with a hatchet face and dark-red curly hair showing under a grey, rolled-brim hat, stood over him, suddenly kicked him in the belly. The miserable traitor — if that's what he was — retched and fell forward, writhing.

The big man held out his right hand towards one of the two silent, gun-hung hombres standing over the downed

4

man. He was handed a Colt, butt first. The redhead cocked the sixgun and leaned over the one on the ground.

'*Hope you had time to enjoy your bribe, you son of a bitch! Because now it's time to pay the piper!*'

He placed the muzzle of the gun to the man's head and pulled the trigger. He half-straightened and fired twice more into the jerking body.

'*Jesus Christ!*'

The words burst unbidden from the watcher's lips, not very loud, but as the echoes of the gunshots died away it seemed to him that he had screamed them. The redhead snapped his head around. 'Who's that?'

The snake man was moving even as one of the others said, 'I never heard nothin', boss.'

'Me, neither.'

The redhead, frowning, still holding the smoking gun as he stood over the body of the traitor, glared around, his gaze travelling as far as the overhanging scrub would allow.

The gun came up and he fired twice.

'*There! There! Christ, are you blind! Get after that son of a bitch and put a bullet in him!*'

The snake man grabbed a slim tree trunk, pulling himself in tight against it, looking back, afraid to move.

Guns blasted but they were shooting in the opposite direction!

Something moved in that section, but it was low and shadow-like — some kind of animal: maybe an ocelot or a young boar. Whatever it was, it could *move!* The men ran in that direction and then came panting back.

'It's OK, boss, just a critter, some kinda wildcat or pig.'

Mr Cordell frowned, holding the six-gun in both hands now. From where he pressed against the tree, the watcher could see it had a large piece broken out of the staghorn butt.

'I *heard* something!' Cordell insisted. 'A voice.'

The two men looked at each other but said nothing. Cordell glanced down at the dead man and kicked him savagely in the ribs at least six times. Then he spat on the body and tossed the gun with the broken butt to the closest of the men, a man with a square face shagged by a jet-black beard.

'Get rid of this garbage. I'll see you back at the ranch.'

'How about we just set fire to the scrub, boss?' the second man said. He was leaner than his companion, but taller and wore a hat with a high crown, making him look like a beanpole. 'That'll take care of Crewe's body an' everythin'.'

'You damn fool! You want to join him, Borden?' The redhead gestured at the dead man. 'There're two hundred mustangs somewhere in this scrub: I aim to round 'em up, use what I can, sell the rest . . . Now, take the body to one of the canyons, a *deep* one, and drop him into it.'

He spun away, large shoulders thrusting aside the brush as he strode off, presumably towards where their horses were tethered.

The snake man hunkered down by his tree until all three — and the body — had gone.

His heart was hammering and his brow was wet with sweat: he had figured he had been squeezed dry hours ago.

Just showed how much he had been affected by the murder he had witnessed.

And he hadn't done a damn thing to prevent it.

2

The Saddlemaker

Most folk in the town of Babylon figured Steve Bannister was not only dull, but also a soft touch.

This, in their opinion, covered a multitude of sins: so what if he never attended church, although he dropped off his wife and daughter there, using that old buckboard that smelled of cured hides and sometimes leather dye. It did not look well surrounded by the brightly painted buggies and fringed surreys, and it was obvious that Linda Bannister was well aware of this and somewhat embarrassed — maybe that was why she gave so generously when the collection plate was passed around. She dressed well, and made sure that pretty seven-year-old daughter, Tess, always looked a picture, with her long sausage-like blonde curls and naturally rosy cheeks, as she ought to, of course. They were tolerably well off, the Bannisters, as he was the only saddle-maker in town and this end of the county. He had a clientele that rode many miles for one of his saddles, or any other leather gear he made: holsters, knife sheaths, saddle-scabbards, harness, purses, wallets — an all-round craftsman.

The Bannisters were a family who kept to themselves but appeared to be quite happy, indeed, a lot happier than some of the rich, highfalutin folks who had a say in running the town and so set the social do's and don'ts.

But, as is always the case, when someone is just a tiny bit off the mainstream, they are the subject of gossip and conjecture.

Then the day two men named Borden and Gann came to town *really* set the tongues wagging.

★   ★   ★

When the bell above the shop door tinkled, Bannister was out the back at his work table, using the half-moon cutting blade on the heavy hide taken from the shoulder section of a huge bull from Kerry Damon's K-D spread.

He swore softly under his breath — Linda and Tess were outside in the flower garden they were nurturing, so he sighed, and called, 'Be with you in a minute.'

He completed the cut and gave the saddle-bag flap a quick, critical scan, wiped his hands on his leather apron and started for the door that led to the shop section.

'Ooops!' He swung aside and picked up a set of oval-lensed spectacles in a wire frame and hooked the arms over his ears, briefly running a hand over his long brown hair as he stepped through the doorway.

There was a matronly woman standing at the counter and she pushed back her veil and gave him a brief smile, sagging jowls trembling slightly.

'Good morning, Mr Bannister. I've come for George's tobacco pouch. I trust you have it ready?'

'All set to go, Mrs Barron.' Bannister was a tall, bearded man, his rolled-up sleeves showing his strong forearms and the beginning of hard biceps. He did all his own skinning and hide selection and tanning: years of such work kept a man in pretty good shape. 'Seeing as it's his sixtieth birthday, I carved his initials on the flap.' He held the polished tan pouch for her to see and she gave a small sigh.

'Oh my, that's lovely, Mr Bannister! So neat and . . . and decorative. But I — I don't know if I have enough to pay for the extra work.'

Wrapping the pouch in tissue paper he said, 'That's all right, Mrs Barron. Accept it as my birthday gift to George. We've spent many hours swapping yarns and he's always good company.'

'Oh, you're a kind man, Mr Bannister. I do appreciate this.' She counted out some coins which he scooped up, smiling, and dropped into the shallow cash drawer.

'Tell him he can stop by a little later if he wants. I just might be able to find a small brandy for him to celebrate his birthday — if he feels the need for a bracer, of course.'

She chuckled. 'I'll tell him. If I know George he'll be down interrupting your work within the hour!' She waved her small package and he went around the counter, held the door for her. 'My very sincere thanks, Mr Bannister.'

'Tell George to have a very good birthday.'

As he closed the door after her, he glanced at two riders walking their mounts slowly past the saddle shop on their way down Main. *Strangers*, he noted automatically, tensed slightly as they seemed to be showing an interest in him, or was it only the display window with an array of his work that had caught their attention?

They moved on, exchanged a word or two, and didn't glance back as they spotted the livery and made their way towards it: another couple of dusty drifters in to slake their thirsts and no doubt see the elephant in the back room of Stacey's Excelsior saloon.

He returned to his workbench, removing the spectacles first, before picking up the edging tool to shave a thin ribbon of leather off the saddle-bag flap he was making.

Linda and Tess came in for lunch and for once they had the meal together without any interruption by customers who often ignored the sign in the window, saying: *Closed for Lunch, 12 noon — 12.30 p.m. daily.*

'And how does your garden grow, Miss Tess?' he enquired, as Linda set a plate of salad and cold beef slices before him.

'My petunias are bigger than Mom's,' the little girl piped, with undisguised pleasure. 'You'll have to come and look at them, Daddy. All sorts of colours and — '

'I have to get this saddle-bag made

for Cam Michaels by tomorrow, sweet-heart.'

Linda cleared her throat and he glanced up. She shook her head slightly, rolled her eyes towards their daughter. 'She's a marvellous little gardener. Her patch is flowering much better than mine . . . you should see it, Steven.'

He took the hint and nodded, smiling. 'But Cam's not one for turning up on time, so, right after lunch we'll go and inspect this blaze of colour: it sounds too good to miss. OK?'

The pleasure that lit up Tess's face, as always, made his heart lurch and he felt the surge of warm affection wash over his entire body.

★ ★ ★

It was mid-afternoon and he had the flap and its gusset in the wooden clamp, the base held down by his thighs, as he stitched the leather with twin saddler's needles, pushing the points through the same hole from either side, then drawing the waxed cord through, pulling it tight enough to make the twine sing. It required concentration and effort to make each stitch exactly the same length and with the same tension so as not to distort the thinner leather of the gusset, and therefore spoil the shape of the finished product.

He looked up once, frowning a little, pausing with the twine pulled halfway through. Then he shrugged and continued — he thought Linda had called. But it wasn't likely — she knew he wouldn't want any interruptions at this stage.

Next moment, he was flinging the clamp and leather aside, lifting a leg swiftly over the workstool and lunging for the door that led to the back yard.

There had been no mistake this time, only it wasn't Linda calling him, it was Tess . . .

He ran around the storeshed to where the gardens were and slowed abruptly. Linda lay on the ground, her clothing torn, her face streaked with blood. Tess was kneeling over her, alternately sobbing and calling his name.

'My God! What's happened?'

'It — it was those two men, Daddy!'

He froze, belly knotted, mouth suddenly parched.

'What men, sweetheart?' His voice sounded thick.

'They-they said to tell you to have a drink with them — for-for old times' sake . . . ' The tear-stained, anguished little face turned upwards and he lunged for her, snatching her up and holding her to his chest.

'It's all right, sweetheart. No one's going to hurt you. I'll see to that.'

'*Daddy! You're hurting!*'

★   ★   ★

He brought the town to a standstill.

Folk walking the streets stopped dead in their tracks. Vehicles rumbling down Main were dragged to an abrupt halt. Everyone in the vicinity stared in total disbelief.

17

Steve Bannister, still wearing his work spectacles and leather apron, strode purposefully down the street, long legs covering the distance rapidly, head erect, jaw jutting, making his beard stand out and bristle. They had never seen him look the way he was now.

Usually a sober, though pleasant face, always polite, helping ladies up on to the boardwalk or down from the stage if he happened to be passing at off-loading time. If he wore a hat, which was rare, he always touched the brim to passing acquaintances, both male and female. No one had ever seen him drunk or heard him raise his voice in anger.

Now — well, folk got out of his way yards ahead of him. His gaze was fixed on the batwings of the Excelsior and he held a *rifle* across his chest. Not only had no one in town seen him with a gun before, but they hadn't even known he owned one.

Now he stepped up on to the four

steps that led to the boardwalk running outside the saloon and slammed into the batwings as if he would wrench them off their hinges.

The racket brought up the heads of every drinker and gambler and saloon girl in the place. Inside, dim though it was, and must seem dimmer to Bannister having just come in out of brilliant sunlight, he raked his hard gaze along the line of drinkers at the bar. He fixed it on the two men he had seen riding past his store earlier when he was saying goodbye to Mrs Barron.

They were expecting him: it was easy to see that by the way they smirked, half-facing him. They turned full-on as he came striding up.

'See you got our message,' the tall one with the long sideburns said, thin lips curling. 'What you drinkin', snake man?'

They were the last coherent words the tall man would speak for a long, long time.

The brass-bound rifle butt came

swinging up and smashed into his face, shattering the jaw, knocking him six feet along the bar. As his legs folded and he fell, the butt crashed into his head and he stretched out, one arm hooked over the brass footrail, his blood dribbling into the floor's sawdust.

The other man, startled, jumped away from the bar, reaching for his gun. Bannister brought the rifle butt up into the man's crotch and he screamed, clawing at himself as his legs folded and started to fall forward. Again the rifle moved in its short, deadly arc, and the man's nose and lips were crushed. A couple of broken teeth spilled to the floor as he fell face-first into the few inches of sodden sawdust.

His gun hand lay pressed against the floor and Bannister smashed the brass-bound butt down on to it, moved back to the first man and his hand lying across the brass footrail.

It received the same treatment. There were white, stunned faces all round. The barkeep, leaning over the counter, glanced at the battered men and slowly lifted his gaze to Bannister's face.

It was set in bleak, stiff lines, the eyes like gun barrels.

'Christ, Steve. What-what the hell d'you think you're doin'?'

Bannister glared back, silently.

'Judas! I mean — *why*? What happened?'

Someone had sent for Ash Temple, the sheriff, and he came striding down the room now, hatless, revealing his thinning pale hair, about Bannister's size, but a few years older. He was wearing his gun and he let a hand casually drop to the butt as he turned his gaze from the bloody men on the saloon floor to the town's saddle-maker.

'Your womenfolk all right, Steve?' the lawman asked, smart enough to know it had to be something bad to have set Bannister off like this. And no one was more important to Bannister than his family.

Steve nodded slightly. 'They jumped

Linda and Tess in the back garden. Roughed up Linda and scared the stuffing outa young Tess.'

There was a murmur of sympathy mixed with anger at his words. Temple's gaze never left Bannister's face.

'They with someone?'

'George Barron and his wife looked in for George's birthday drink. Mrs Barron's caring for them and George went for Doc Penney.'

The lawman sighed. 'Well, he's got some extra work here . . . you know these *hombres*?'

Bannister shook his head.

'How you know where to find 'em?'

'One of 'em told Tess to tell me to come have a drink for old times' sake — ' Bannister stopped, obviously having said more then he meant to.

'Then, seems at least one of 'em knew you from some other time.'

'I've never seen either one before, Ash. Not as I recall, leastways.'

Temple studied Bannister's face, reached out and gently took the rifle from him. 'Why don't we go down to the office and see if we can figure this out?'

Bannister hesitated, then nodded.

'What about these two, Ash?' the barkeep demanded gesturing to the bloody men on the floor.

'Doc Penney'll be down. I'll send Jack Tatum to make sure he comes.'

The sound of their footsteps was muffled by the layer of damp sawdust. As soon as the batwings swung closed after them, the big bar room exploded into sound.

'Can't believe Steve Bannister done that!'

'No, not sleepy ol' Steve.'

'By hell, he was wide awake when he fixed the wagon on them two sons of bitches!'

'Christ! I owe him for a bridle from last month. I hope he don't come after me like that!'

'Idiot! Steve don't worry none about the money: it's his family that's important to him. Somethin' happens to them and — well, you seen how riled he can get.'

'Yeah, but *Steve!* Of all people. I just can't swallow it, even though I seen it with my own eyes.'

'What I'd like to know is who sent these bastards after him — and why!'

Twenty pairs of wondering eyes turned to the speaker.

That was a good question.

3

Witness

Sheriff Ash Temple placed Bannister's rifle in the rack beside his wall cupboard and the saddler smiled thinly.

'Hope you're not aiming to keep that, Ash. Had that old Henry a long time.'

'It'll be safe there.' Temple sat down, took out a pipe from a desk drawer, packed it from a leather humidor Bannister had made for him, decorated with carved acanthus leaves, and lit up. 'One hard *hombre*.'

Bannister arched his eyebrows.

'I'm talkin' about you, Steve. Folk hereabouts think you'll jump up on a chair if you see a mouse and — well, look what you did.'

'A mouse wouldn't even scare Linda — or Tess. But those sonuvers did, and they hurt Linda as well.'

'And you hurt 'em back, but good.' He lifted a hand to cut off Bannister's reply. 'I know you and your family well enough to accept what you did, because I know you wouldn't've got so rough for any other reason than someone had hurt 'em, but I need to know more. There's a why in there someplace and I want it explained.'

Temple's hard eyes were like gimlets in his tough face, settling on Bannister's bearded features. The sheriff gestured with his pipe. 'You can take off them useless glasses if you want.'

'Useless?' Bannister was wary now, but removed the spectacles.

'You recollect they got knocked off and busted when Jimbo Reed's hoss bolted and you grabbed the bridle? Jimbo was grateful enough to have your glasses fixed — though I recollect now you didn't want him to do it — but he did. An' the eye-doctor told him they was just plain glass. I told Jimbo you likely wore 'em to protect your eyes while you were workin', rather than for seein' better. But they could be some kind of disguise, too.' Bannister remained silent. 'Wasn't the first time I got interested in you, Steve. You're a fine saddlemaker and leather-worker, but I've been a lawman for over twenty years and I've seen a lot of hard men in my day. I suspicioned you were a damn sight harder than you tried to make out.'

'You never asked.'

Temple shrugged. 'You're a law-abidin' family man. If you had somethin' in your past you were runnin' from, it was no business of mine . . . unless you broke the law in my bailiwick.'

Bannister moved a little uneasily on his chair, glanced briefly through the dusty window. 'I hope Linda's all right . . . '

'You know Doc Penney's good — and that nurse of his, Fran someone, she's great with kids — Linda and Tess're OK.'

'We could do this later, Ash.'

'No. Not the way you beat-up on those fellers. I've got to get a clearer picture of you, Steve. And now.'

Bannister obviously didn't like it but finally he nodded.

'C'mon, Steve! You know what I want and I'm losin' patience.'

Bannister saw he couldn't push Temple much more, despite their five-year friendship. He tried to settle more comfortably in the straight-back chair.

'I was outrider for Boyd Derrick, the BeeDee spread outside of Tucson. About ten, eleven years back.'

'I know of Derrick — big-time cattleman.'

'Now he is, but he was still growing at the time I'm talking about. I liked outriding. A man could be his own boss most of the times, checking fence lines, pastures, straying cattle, repairing line-shacks and so on. I heard some missing cattle had been seen heading for San Lividio and I was on my way to check it out when a rattler killed my horse and left me afoot at the edge of the Solitario Flats.'

'Better places to be without a hoss.'

'Lots better. Anyway, I was resting in some scrub, heard voices, and when I looked through the brush I saw four men, three on their feet, the fourth on his knees, pleading with a redhead not to kill him. But that's just what the redhead did: murdered the man in cold blood, then kicked him and spat on him. Feller named Crewe, I learned later.'

Temple's pipe had gone out now, but he was concentrating so hard on Bannister's words he didn't notice.

'You actually witnessed this redhead killing the other feller?'

'Yeah. They cleared off, taking the body with 'em.'

'And you stayed put.'

'Told you my horse ran off after the rattler bit it. My guns were still in the saddle-bags and scabbard. I came up on a round-up camp and borrowed a horse to get me to San Lividio. First

29

man I see in the plaza was the red-haired killer.' He paused, Temple frowning as he leaned forward a little. 'He was walking towards the saloon with the town's sheriff. Feller named Redman at that time.'

Temple's eyes narrowed. 'Mort Redman.' He practically spat the word. 'Locked him up for graft and bribery and runnin' white women across the Border into *mañana* land. Someone slid a home-made knife between his ribs in the prison yard. Good riddance.'

'Well, I'd heard a few things about him and figured he'd be the last man to tell about what I'd seen, so I rode to Tucson where there was a US Marshals' office, feller named Bronco Madigan, and told him my story. I knew Madigan was a straight-shooter and tougher than a brace of grizzlies.'

'Yeah, whatever happened to him? Never hear about him these days. He was one mighty tough *hombre*.'

'He disappeared. Heard they're still searching now and again. But at that time he moved fast. He knew who the red-haired rancher was: Rance Cordell. For a long time he'd been suspected of running an outlaw bunch, raiding stage coaches and express offices, holding-up banks. Madigan had me write out a sworn statement before a judge and had it notarized and tied up and sealed like it was the Declaration of Independence. Then he handed me a court order requiring me to give evidence against Cordell, or I'd be charged with obstructing a murder investigation.'

He paused, waiting for some reaction from Temple, who spread his hands. 'Well? What did you expect? You were an eye-witness. They had Cordell cold after all this time, but only if you testified.'

Bannister frowned. 'I was only about twenty at the time, remember, Ash. I'd heard a lot about this Cordell while I was in Tucson and — well, I guess I was scared. He was a mighty powerful man, had all kinds of connections with politicians and so on. And those two fellers who'd been with him at the murder scene were still missing.'

'Madigan wanted to nail Cordell — he wouldn't've been worried much about the other two.'

'I knew that, damnit! But I felt like I was outa my depth: me, just a kid, going up against some big-time crook like Cordell? The rooming-house where I was staying was burned down: the fire started under my window . . . '

He paused, once again remembering that first terror as the flames surged up and cracked the smudged glass. Then the choking, blinding smoke, the reek of coal oil as he tried to find his way out of the blazing room; the shadow that came at him out of the smoke, a club in one hand, a six-gun in the other.

'Shoulda kept your mouth shut, dummy!'

The club whistled towards his head and he ducked, shoulder hitting the wall. He felt the heat through the scorching timber and the club smashed into the wood an inch from his skull.

The man cursed and brought up the six-gun.

Bannister, half-blinded, choking, pretty much afraid, kicked out, felt his boot connect with the killer's shin. The man howled, staggered, the swinging six-gun missed by a whisker and he knew then the man didn't want to shoot — no gunshots, just a battered, burned body to be found lying amongst the charred timbers.

Like hell!

He brought up a knee, reacting by instinct, and felt it connect with the man's face. His fists clubbed down on to the back of the exposed neck and the man stretched out at his feet. He left the club (that would burn) but took the six gun, ramming it into his belt as he groped his way out, found an exit at the rear.

A charred body was found after the fire was finally extinguished and, as it was outside his room, they reckoned it was him.

He felt a strange sense of freedom: they had their body now, and hopefully that would keep them off his neck and give him a chance to hide out someplace.

'Nice move,' Ash Temple said, but there was still a lawman's disapproval in his tone.

'Didn't work for long. I guess when the feller with the club never turned up they started to put things together. I was in another town by then and a horse I was using was found without its head down by a creek back of the livery where I kept it. The head turned up later: in my bed at the rooming-house where I was staying.'

Ash Temple smiled crookedly. 'Someone was trying to tell you somethin' — you weren't dumb enough not to figure that, were you?'

'Oh, I figured it all right: give evidence and I was dead.'

'You'd've been dead before you could give it.'

'That's what I reckoned, even told Madigan I could've been mistaken about what I'd seen.' Bannister shook his head slowly. 'He damn near killed me! Threw me in jail and beat the crap out of me. Know what he said? 'They're gonna kill you if you try to give evidence, boy, and I'm surely gonna kill you if you turn chickenshit on me at this stage'.'

'The proverbial rock and the hard place, huh?' Temple seemed mildly amused. 'And typical Bronco Madigan.'

'Hell, I was more scared of Madigan than Cordell! But he said he'd do a deal: I give evidence that would put Cordell away for a long time or maybe even earn him a death sentence, though he doubted that, with the kind of lawyers Cordell and his friends could hire, and Madigan swore he'd protect me and any family I had for as long as necessary. He didn't make a big thing about it, just said 'You got my word on that', and somehow I knew he meant it.'

'So, in the end, you gave evidence?'

Bannister nodded. 'Cordell got twenty-five years in Yuma. His friends had saved him from a noose, but I knew they wouldn't give up trying to find me. Before he disappeared, Madigan fixed things so I had a new name, a whole new life — making saddles is pretty far from punching cows. I'd always been a loner and liked it, but when I met Linda' — he shrugged — 'knew I'd be twice as vulnerable but . . . we sure hit it off, Linda and me.'

'Madigan kept his word?'

'Yeah. Then he disappeared, but the marshals still watched out for me, moved me around quite a bit in case Cordell's men got a line on me. Tess came along and Linda didn't want to keep moving house every few years. She wanted to put down roots. We figured we'd earned it and that Cordell's men had lost our trail. Eventually, the marshals agreed and let us choose where we wanted to go — but I wouldn't tell them where. I didn't want *anyone* to know but ourselves.'

'So you came here to Babylon, and

had five years without a problem — till now.'

'Yeah. Looks like they've tracked us down again and we'll have to be moving on.'

Temple studied him briefly and Bannister frowned.

'Bronco Madigan show you how to take care of yourself?'

'He did. Taught me about guns. Thought I was pretty good in a fight, but he made me look like a choirboy, showed me stuff I'd never even heard about. Once or twice it came in handy.'

Like the time he was saddling his horse in a livery stall and a man dropped out of the loft, a 'breed, who came at him with a knife. Madigan had showed him how to step inside the knife arm, use his own body to force it aside, and if possible, pin it against a wall.

A narrow livery stall was ideal. He pinned the 'breed's arm, stomped on the man's instep, his weight holding the killer just where he wanted him. Then he smashed his knuckles into the dirty Adam's apple. The man choked, frantic now. Bannister turned the knife arm back, the blade entering just under the arch of the ribs, driving up into the heart . . .

'Madigan knew a lot of dirty tricks and used 'em.'

'Yeah. He had a reputation for rough stuff. Reckon what you did today in the Excelsior had a touch of Madigan in it. Bronco was a mighty tough man, had his own ideas about justice.'

'How about you, Ash?'

Temple tapped out the cold dottle in his pipe and glanced up. 'Well, we been friends a few years, Steve, pretty good friends, but — I think you oughta move out of Babylon and take your family with you. Sooner the better.'

★ ★ ★

But it wasn't that easy.

Linda had been hurt by her attackers. Nothing sexual, or crippling, but she had been punched and kicked — even Tess had a black eye and sore arm which still bore the red marks from where it had been twisted.

With the normal resilience of a child, she was fully recovered already, but Linda had badly bruised ribs and was still recovering from the shock.

'I wouldn't like to see her travelling by horse or even buckboard for at least a week, Steve,' Dr Penney said. He was twenty years older than Bannister, a man dedicated to his work, so Steve listened.

'How about a stagecoach, Doc?'

'Slightly better than a buckboard, but not all that much. Steve, Linda has had a pretty bad beating. I really would like to keep an eye on her for a few more days — minimum.

'You know we've got some trouble, Doc? Yeah, figured Ash had mentioned it. Sooner we clear town and get ourselves some other hidey-hole the better.'

Penney frowned, rubbing at his

drooping moustache thoughtfully. 'Suppose — I have a sister at Dander's Crossing. Our mother was ill for a long time before she died and we had a special surrey built, very well sprung, enclosed with leather wrap-around blinds for bad weather, a reclining seat because Mother had to lie down on even short journeys. The ideal form of transport, Steve. I'm sure Ida would be pleased to drive up and take Linda and Tess back with her.'

'That's fine, Doc. I need to stay on here long enough to arrange the sale of the business — feller from Stedman Saddles in Tucson has been interested for some time. I'll be glad to pay your sister for her trouble until I can find somewhere to move to more permanently.'

'If I know Ida, she won't take any money, but that can be sorted out later. I'll send a wire to her right away.'

When Penney had gone and the nurse, Fran Whittaker, had left Linda's room, Bannister told his bruised and pale-looking wife about the arrangements. Her hand came out from under the sheets and clasped his. She looked up into his drawn face.

'I don't want us to be separated, Steven! Tess won't, either.'

He patted her hand. 'Hon, it's the best way for now. We have to get out of town before they send in someone else to replace those two who did this to you.'

Her grey eyes searched his face. 'I heard about what you did. I-I'm as surprised as anybody else! I knew you could be hard, but . . . not like that. I'm not disapproving, but it did come as something of a shock.'

'Don't worry about it. I'll get in touch with Stedman's and they can send a man out to put a value on the business. I'll accept whatever they reckon is fair.'

'Oh, it's not right, Steven! All these years you've put into building up the business to what it is!'

'It *is* a business, Linda, but that's all.

You can put a price on it, but there's no price you can put on your life. Or Tess's. Now you rest and prepare yourself to go with Doc's sister, Ida. I'll break the news to Tess and start thinking about places where we can go and stay safe.'

If there is such a place!

4

Freedom day

The warden looked up from the legal papers he was holding, glaring at the man in prison rags standing on the other side of the desk flanked by armed guards.

He was a tall, gangling man, with close-cropped sandy-coloured hair, sprinkled with grey. His face was gaunt, bony, the eyes sunken, with dark shadows under the sockets.

The warden sat back, still holding the papers.

'I don't know how you managed to arrange this, Cordell, but I do not approve of your release, no matter how strict the board stresses the conditions must be.'

'Well, I'm not about to look a gift horse in the mouth, Warden,' Cordell

43

said, with a touch of a smirk. His voice was rough and it seemed to be an effort for him to speak.

'I'll bet you're not! Must've cost a small fortune to get the fix in for this result.'

'Aw, now, Warden, why d'you say that? You know I've been a model prisoner these last nine years or so. I'm a changed man! OK, I admit I lost my temper with that damn fool, but if someone had cost you thousands of dollars because he let a herd of your prime breeder cows run into a bog through plain, *stupid* negligence, wouldn't you be kinda mad? Mad enough to put a bullet in him?'

'Don't come that act with me, Cordell! We both know why you murdered Crewe and it had nothing to do with bogged cows.'

Rance Cordell's thin lips curled slightly and he nodded towards the papers shaking in the warden's hands. 'Well, that's all over an' done with, Warden. The courts had their say about that and now, after three tries, the parole board has finally granted me my release. You got it right there in your hand.'

'Under damn strict conditions which I, personally, will check on to make sure they're adhered to!'

'Now, Warden, you know you don't have any right to do that. The court's appointed its watchdogs and they'll — '

'Shut up! Don't you quote what's legal and what's not, to me, you murdering son of a bitch!'

Cordell's smile faded a little, then came back in full smirk. 'If you could just sign my release form, Warden . . . ? One of my attorneys is downstairs I understand and if I have to call him . . .'

The Warden grabbed a pen, overfilled the nib, and scrawled a blotchy signature across the form, flung it so it skidded off the desk and fell on the floor at Cordell's feet.

'Pick it up, if you want it, then get out of my sight . . . I'll be damned glad to be rid of you, Cordell.'

The warden turned and looked out the window at the grey, bleak day, hands locked together behind his back, opening and closing in agitation. He didn't even turn around when the door slammed as Cordell and his guards exited.

By God, it galled him to have to turn loose that scheming, cold-blooded bastard out into an unsuspecting world!

★ ★ ★

There was no attorney waiting: Cordell had known that when he threatened the warden, but it had worked, hadn't it? Got the parole papers officially signed and now here he was on the next step to freedom. To hell with the 'strict conditions': there was always a way around such things, and he still had a lot of money at his disposal. *He better had! Or someone else would have their brains blown out!*

It was drizzling rain when Cordell

and his escort arrived at the main gate. The gate guard, Quigley, looked pleased when he told Cordell, now wearing his old rolled-brim hat — it was too large now his hair had been cut so close to his skull — and baggy clothes. 'Transport wagon left a mite early, Cordell. Guess you'll just have to walk to town!'

'Now that's no surprise. But I'd crawl, as long as I was moving away from this manure heap, and the rats in it.'

The guard sniggered, closed the port in the main gate with a crash. 'Mebbe a cougar'll get you on the way! There's been two of 'em hangin' around out there lately, lookin' for scraps an' garbage — figure you qualify, Cordell!'

I'll remember you, Quigley! By hell I will!

Cordell started walking along the muddy trail, already starting to shiver as the rain soaked his old clothes. They stank from long storage, were partly rotted, but, by God, he would be wearing broadcloth and velvet and silk within a couple of days when he got back to his ranch, or he would know the reason why.

He stopped abruptly, heart hammering, as a man stepped out from behind a tree, directly in his path, his slicker gleaming with the rain. Just for a moment, in the half-light, it had looked like the rain-wet coat of a big cat.

'Sorry about the weather, Mr Cordell. Got a spare slicker in my saddlebags back there if you want it.' He gestured to a line of bushes and Cordell could just make out two horses tethered there.

'Then get it, you damn fool! Who the hell are you anyway?'

'Chick Borden. You might recall my young brother Mitch worked for you before . . . ' He let his voice trail off and gestured briefly towards the grey bulk of the jail now some hundred yards behind the released prisoner — 'he . . . died.'

'I can't remember every damn fool ever worked for me that long ago.

Where the hell is my slicker?'

Chick Borden helped him into the ill-fitting garment, refraining from mentioning how much weight Cordell had lost.

'Damn useless thing! Letting in more water than it's keeping out!'

'Sorry, Mr Cordell. They told me it was your size.' Cordell glared, swore. Chick cleared his throat. 'Mr Langdon sent me to meet you — your attorney?'

'Christ, I'm not senile, even if I look it! I know who Langdon is. Why didn't he come himself?'

He frowned when Borden grinned, rain catching on his bristly jowls and trickling down his neck above the slicker.

'He's kinda busy, he said.'

Cordell swore. 'Too damn busy to see that that lousy warden signed the papers without all the insults he threw at me? By God, he'll be lucky if he's still my attorney ten minutes after I see him again!'

'Aw, mebbe I should've explained better, Mr Cordell. The counsellor's

49

busy finalizing a few things on your behalf, I b'lieve, was the way he put it.'

'What things, damnit?'

'Well, he said to tell you he hopes to have a coming-out present for you by the time you get to see him. Said you'd know what he means.'

Cordell had stiffened: even under the bulky slicker his rigid posture was noticeable. He stared hard at Borden who was grinning now.

'There's only one thing I can think of that I'd like for a coming-out present.'

'Yeah, he said that.'

'Well?'

'And that's it, Mr Cordell. He's tracked down the son of a bitch who got you put in jail.'

Cordell didn't move, his face set in blank lines. Then he reached up, took off his hat and flung it high in the air, prison-ravaged face lifted to the rain, uncaring that the water ran down inside the slicker like a miniature flood.

'Man! What a beautiful day, ain't it? Just so goddamn *beautiful*!'

50

* ★ ★

Sheriff Temple said he would send Deputy Jack Tatum to ride along with Doc Penney's sister's surrey.

'Thanks, Ash, but I'll go myself.'

The lawman frowned slightly. 'Jack's a good man, Steve.'

'I know. But not good enough for me to sit back chewing my nails while Linda and Tess travel to Dander's Crossing. I have to see them down there safely myself, Ash. Then I'll come back and start things moving to get rid of the business.'

'I savvy how you feel, I guess. If that's the way you want it, OK. Jack's got town patrol tonight. I'll have him keep an extra eye on your place.'

Bannister thanked him and took the rifle the sheriff handed him.

'You seem kinda partial to that gun.'

'Boyd Derrick gave it to me — was his own at one time. I kinda hoped some of his luck would rub off on me.'

'Best watch the ammo you use in it.

Nowadays it's more powerful than the old stuff this was made for.'

'Had the breech strengthened by a gunsmith a few years back — traded him a new set of saddle-bags.'

Temple gave one of his rare smiles. 'Yeah, you kinda fit into this country well, don't you, Steve? You and Linda and Tess. Damn shame you've got to uproot this way.'

Soberly, Bannister told him it had happened before. 'This'll be the third or fourth time. I don't keep count but Linda does.'

'Yeah. I figure it'd likely be worse for a woman, a mother especially, to have to reorganize her life every so often.'

'Maybe this'll be the last time it's necessary . . . What's wrong?'

The sheriff looked at him steadily, shook his head briefly. 'Maybe this'll be the hardest time of all.'

'Which means . . . ?'

'Tess doin' so well at school, Linda with her own ladies' group at the church an' — aw, hell! Forget that.

Steve, I guess I've been kinda holdin' out on you a little.'

'Little or big, holding-out is still that, Ash.' Bannister's voice was clipped, his mouth drawn into a tight line.

The lawman nodded, embarrassed. 'Wire came through earlier, general information for law officers. Marshals put 'em out now and again when they figure it's important enough.'

'I'd like to know, too! If it don't take you all damn day to tell me.'

Temple's eyes flashed, but briefly. 'Well, seems Cordell was released on parole yesterday.'

Bannister was very still, silent, his gaze on Temple's face, but obviously seeing something a lot further away than the lawman.

'How the hell could that be? He was in for *murder!*'

Temple sighed. 'Money, Steve. Money and power and reachin' the good ol' boys in the right place at the right time. He's applied a couple times before. They refused him and that'll look good on their records. This time, they said yes and laid out strict conditions — which no one'll bother with, likely, but who can blame the parole board for that? They only make the recommendations; up to someone else to see they're followed.'

'Where is he?'

Temple shrugged. 'Likely back at his ranch. His half-brother, Mace McQueen, has been runnin' things, strictly legal far as anyone can tell. But a set of books showing everythin's soap-suds-clean means nothin' to these people. They can write 'em up anyway they like and you can bet your britches they'll be good enough to stand in court.'

'And you were gonna send one of your deputies to ride shotgun on my family! After what's already happened!'

'Yeah, I know, Steve. I-I figured you had enough worries, but I should've reckoned you'd want to escort them yourself. I would, too, in your place.'

'Anything else you've been keeping as

a surprise? I mean, I'm all excited now, looking forward to finding out just how much my life is gonna change . . . by the goddamn hour, seems like!'

'Now take it easy. I shouldn't've held back. I made a judgement and it was wrong. I apologize, Steve. How about I have Tatum ride with you?'

'*I'll* take care of my family: they're my responsibility.'

Temple sighed as Bannister strode towards the door. 'You know I'm here if you need — '

The slamming door cut off his last words.

★   ★   ★

They made the drive by night.

The doctor's sister was older then he was, her grey hair pulled back into a bun behind her head. She had a lined, sour-looking face, but was a pleasant woman to speak to, a widow of eleven years. She assured Bannister she didn't mind in the least coming all this way.

'Well, be best if you rest up now, ma'am, and we'll get going early in the morning. You like to nominate a time? I mean, don't wanta get you outa bed too early.'

She was dressed in baggy old work trousers and a check blouse. She placed work-worn hands on her ample hips. 'I'll nominate a time, yes. You get your wife loaded into the surrey with your little girl, and we'll start back right away.'

'Aw, now listen, Miz Farnham, I don't want to push you — '

'Young man, I can cut and split a cord of wood faster than two hungry roustabouts, then ride five miles to my pastures and round-up and brand half my herd while they're still wipin' sweat from their brows. They'll be snorin' in the barn while I'm in my kitchen bakin' the week's supply of bread and biscuits, even a fancy cake if I feel so inclined. And after that — '

Scowling at the grinning doctor, Bannister held up a hand. 'All right, ma'am! I see I was mistaken thinking you might care for a good night's sleep before making the return journey.'

'Sooner we get started the better,' she cut in. 'We'll have your family snug in bed before daylight and no one'll know they've even left town.' She paused and with a faint quzzical smile asked, 'Will you be stayin' over, or will you be starting right back?'

'I'll start back.'

'Sure you won't fall asleep in the saddle . . . ?'

'Ma'm, you don't mind me saying, you're kinda pushing things.'

Doc Penney chuckled as Bannister sighed and nodded several times. 'I'll go help the nurse with my wife.'

★   ★   ★

The rain had cleared and the stars were bright and cold, throwing an eerie light along the twisting trail to Dander's Crossing.

Bannister rode back and forth restlessly, spurring on ahead, checking out the country, then coming back to his station slightly to the rear of the enclosed surrey, with Linda strapped into the reclining seat, Tess asleep with her head in Ida Farnham's lap.

They stopped to make coffee well after midnight, both Bannister and the older woman feeling the need for some kind of bracer but neither ready to admit it.

'I was going to bring a jug of my apple cider, but seeing as a child was along — '

'Maybe you'll gimme a snifter before I start back.'

'Maybe I will and maybe I won't. We'll see.'

He grinned and touched a hand in mock salute to the curl-brim of his hat, silhouetted briefly against the stars.

Then he wheeled away abruptly and she heard the rifle slide out of the scabbard, a metallic sound as he worked the lever.

'Who are you and what d'you want?'

Bannister called, staring off to the left of the small fire.

'Hey, easy! I-I'm Boots Larsen. Makin' for Babylon, camped for the night over yonder ridge when I smelled your coffee. I'm about out of everythin' by way of grub, but I run outa coffee first, three-four days ago.'

'Ride back to your camp, Larsen. There's no coffee for you here.'

'Now just a minute, Mr Bannister!'

He ignored the widow's outraged interruption, watching the barely seen shape of the man out there. He lifted the rifle and triggered a shot over the man's head.

'Judas priest! What the hell you think you're doin'?'

'Ride out!'

'Gimme a chance, dammit! You're *the* most unfriendly cuss I've struck in fifteen years of driftin'!'

'Panhandlin' every day of 'em, I'll bet. Not interested, Larsen. And my next shot'll either take you outta the saddle or bring down your horse.'

'Christ! Ah, the hell with you, you damn Piker!'

They heard the horse race away and then the sounds dimmed as he crossed the ridge.

'Was that necessary?' Ida Farnham asked bitterly.

'It was. You put out the fire and get ready to move. I'll just ride on and see that ranny does have a camp over there and that he stays in it.'

The woman felt the knot in her stomach slowly unravel as she heard Linda asking weakly what was the trouble and Tess calling for her mother.

Yes. Bannister was right: it was necessary.

She lifted the reins and started the surrey moving again as Bannister rode back.

'He's camped over there, all right, alone, and with a mighty lean outfit.'

'Then maybe we should offer — '

'No, ma'am. It *looks* all right. We'll just keep going and I'll check the back trail every now and again.'

'Of course. It's the wisest thing to do.'

★ ★ ★

The rest of the journey was uneventful and there was a hint of grey in the east by the time Linda was settled into a new bed and Tess was sleeping, sucking her thumb on Ida's horsehair sofa.

'I'm very much obliged, Miz Farnham.'

'My name's Ida, and you'd better get some rest before you fall out of the saddle.'

'I will after I get back to Babylon. Have to be there in case Stedman sends a man in to inspect my shop.'

★ ★ ★

But there was no representative from Stedman's waiting when Bannister rode into town, well after noon, and swaying in the saddle with fatigue.

And it wouldn't have mattered if

Stedman's man was there or not to inspect the saddle shop.

Because there was no saddle shop.

Only a heap of charred timber and crumbling stacks of hides, some still smouldering.

5

Only the Start

'Nothing we could do to save it, Steve. The town was mostly asleep. Tatum was coming off duty around two, two-thirty, thought he saw a glow over Main and heard a crackling. He ran back and there she was. Bigger bonfire than we've ever had on the Fourth of July.'

Gaunt and haggard, Bannister glanced across the law office to where Jack Tatum sat at his own small desk, really only a scarred old disused card table from the Excelsior, saved from the trash heap.

'Didn't see anyone hanging around?' Bannister asked. 'They usually stick around to watch, fellers who burn buildings.'

'I've heard that, and I did a quick check, but mostly I was trying to raise the alarm, get the fire squad out and workin'.' Tatum swung his large head with its thick curls of steel-grey hair. 'They broke all records gettin' there, but it had too good a hold. I feel bad about it, Steve. I had a close look on my rounds, didn't see nothin' suspicious, no smell of coal oil or anythin'. Sonuver musta waited till I come back here to sign-off.'

'You did what you could, Jack.' Bannister shifted his gaze to the sheriff. 'These bastards are hitting hard and fast, Ash.'

Temple nodded slowly. 'Yeah. Has to be Cordell's crowd. Kinda set things up for him, like a comin'-out party.'

'That's what I figure.'

'Hell, I guess it has to be that way, but you *sure* he's behind it, Steve? I mean, could it maybe've been an accident? Lamp left burnin' or — '

'I'm sure, Jack. Maybe he didn't give orders to rough-up Linda and scare Tess, or burn the shop, but McQueen's been running the spread and he'd fix something like that, just to show he was on the ball, celebrate Cordell's parole.'

'Long memory.' Tatum sounded mildly doubtful.

'That's Cordell. No one messes with him and gets away with it. I've had some hassles over the years since he went to Yuma — from his friends, looking for me. Never managed to catch anyone, but I knew all along they were working for Cordell. He can't afford to let me live forever, not after standing up in court and telling the judge how I saw him murder that ranny. He's gotta save face and he won't stop till he does.'

Tatum blew out his cheeks, scratched at his bushy moustache. 'Helluva thing to live with.'

'I'll give you no argument there. Well, nothing I can do now. Had some insurance, mostly on the building, but I'll get nothing for all the tanning ponds I built, or the stretching frames or drying racks and so on. I'll send a wire to Stedman's, and then turn-in: I need some sleep.'

'Use one of the cells if you want,' the sheriff offered. 'No one locked up right now.'

'Thanks, Ash, I'll do that. Where're those two who beat up on Linda?'

Temple looked steadily and calmly at his set face. 'In Doc Penney's special lock-up room out back of his infirmary. Ankles chained to the beds that're bolted to the floor. One has his jaw all wired-up, so he can't speak — other won't even tell us his name, and he's in a mighty lot of pain.'

'Good.'

As Bannister left, Tatum said, 'Been a quiet feller for all the years he's lived here, but you see his face, Ash? I tell you, I wouldn't want to be the scum who set that fire if ever Steve Bannister catches up with him.'

'And he will,' Temple said quietly. 'Just hope he doesn't find him in my bailiwick. I went easy on him for what he did to those snakes who beat up Linda, but I reckon whoever set that fire ain't gonna get any further than

Babylon's Boot Hill if Steve finds him. I can't bend the law all the damn time, not even for him.'

Bannister did find the man, in the bar of the Excelsior, just before noon the next day.

Or was it the other way round?

Like this:

He slept all right in the bunk in one of Temple's cells and had breakfast with the sheriff. Then he went down to the remains of the store, a few spots still with faint eddies of smoke, and stared for a time, nodding to passers-by who offered their sympathy.

Then he rolled his sleeves up above the elbows and began searching through the rubble. He saved a few tools that could be put back into use after a little attention, half-a-dozen bottles of dye and a deep can of leather dressing that had somehow escaped the flames. Out back, he figured he could salvage a few hides, in part, but what was the use?

He wouldn't be able to return to

leather work or saddle-making now: anyone in that trade would be quickly checked out by Cordell's men in their search for him.

No, he'd have to find another way of making a living.

So he simply walked away from the mess, washed-up behind the jail and dressed in a new set of trousers, shirt and vest sent along by Mitchell Cape from the general store — no charge.

He was parched, mouth as dry as that time in the badlands when he had first laid eyes on Cordell. He knew it was inner tension and apprehension: he was on the run again. None of the men looking for him would be waving a flag or anything else that might give him warning: he was running from ruthless, face-less killers.

And his family had to run with him.

That really riled him. *He* was the one Cordell wanted, but Linda and Tess were in just as much danger, simply because they were *his* wife and child.

What kind of scum fought his battles

that way? Targetting innocent women and children?

By hell, he could do with a drink . . .

So he went to Stacey's Excelsior and ordered a whiskey with a beer chaser. Washing down the good red-eye — Stacey never served his friends from the bar stock — with beer that chilled his throat, he set down the glass and took out tobbaco and papers. When the cigarette was built, he patted his pockets on the new shirt — and, of course, there were no vestas.

Then a match flared and came towards the cigarette. He sucked down smoke, exhaled, waved it clear and looked at the man who had given him a light.

Big feller, fortyish, tough-looking, regular trail clothes, ragged black hair — but a stranger to Bannister.

'Smoke always goes well with a coupla drinks, eh?'

Bannister nodded. 'Thanks. New shirt, and I forgot to drop some vestas in the pocket. Buy you a beer?'

'Ah, no thanks. Had a few, waitin' around.'

'Looking for work?'

'Nah. Got a job. Been waitin' for you to show up.'

Steve had the cigarette halfway to his mouth, stopped the movement. His eyes pinched down as he studied the other more closely — no, he was still a stranger.

'I don't know you, friend.'

'No, we've never met. But I seen you once, long time ago. In the Phoenix court. You were givin' evidence, no name, and you were wearin' a floursack hood. Law's idea of protectin' your identity, I guess.'

Bannister was standing straight now. 'Then how the hell could you recognize me now?'

The man smiled, tapped the side of his big nose, the big pores clogged with trail dirt — or ash! 'I just asked the barkeep to give me the high-sign when the feller who used to own that store that burned down came in.'

'And you knew I was the same one gave evidence in the Phoenix court all of ten years ago?'

The man continued to smile and nodded smugly. Bannister's eyes dropped down, and he saw the six-gun on the man's hip: it was a well-used Colt.

And there was a piece broken out of the stag butt, on the inside arc . . .

Bannister looked deeply into those mocking eyes. 'You're the one gave Cordell the gun.'

'No. He borrowed it from my brother, now deceased, thanks to Bronco Madigan! After Rance got out, he sent me to look you up, but your store was empty. Knew I had to do somethin' to grab your attention.'

'So you burned it down, you son of a bitch!'

Bannister's voice was raised now and his words and tone brought a blanket of silence over the big room. All eyes turned towards Bannister and the man he was confronting.

'Well, I have to give you a message

from Mr Cordell, you see. Oh, better make it formal, I guess: my name's Borden and — '

Bannister hit him, using the heavy beer glass. Liquid sprayed as it crumpled Borden's hat and bounced off his head. He floundered along the bar. The stiff felt of the hat had taken some of the sting out of the blow and Borden shook his head, blinking, back-pedalled as Bannister came after him, fists up and swinging.

A blow caught him on the side of the jaw and drinkers scattered as Borden rolled on to a table, upsetting it. He crashed to the floor amongst glasses and cards and a broken chair. He came up swinging the remains of that chair. Bannister swiftly raised his left arm. The legs beat it down. Borden jabbed the splintered remains of the legs at his face. Bannister weaved and ducked, came up inside the man's arms and hammered his midriff.

Borden rolled away, felt the edge of the bar bite into his back. As another blow snapped his head to the side, he saw the bottles on the bar, snatched one up by the neck and smashed it on the zinc edge. The jagged glass slashed air in front of Bannister's face. He dodged and ducked again and, as Borden lunged forward, rammed his head into the man's midriff. It stopped Borden in his tracks, breath gusting from him. He looked as if he might throw-up.

Bannister strode in, fists swinging and hammering the man along the bar, men jumping aside hurriedly. Borden was mighty groggy, legs rubbery, rolling in his efforts to deaden some of the power in those punishing blows. There was a stack of clean glasses on the counter. He lunged for it, used his left arm to sweep the glasses off in a glittering swirl towards Bannister.

Steve ducked, lifting his arms instinctively, battering hurtling glasses aside. Borden lunged in, big fists connecting with the saddler's chest, ramming him back against the bar. Borden used his weight to pin him there, fists blurring as they battered Bannister's mid-section — and lower.

Steve felt his legs going and before they did he brought one up with what strength he could manage. It was hard and it skidded off Borden's thigh, but it made him stumble. Bannister clung to the edge of the bar and kicked. His boot toe hacked Borden's left kneecap and the leg folded as he yelled in pain. His right hand swiftly reached for the six-gun with the broken stag butt.

Men who had been crowding in to get a closer look at the fight suddenly scattered, someone yelling, '*Gun!*'

Unarmed, Bannister knew he was a dead man.

Then Stacey yelled, 'Steve!' and the bar's sawn-off shotgun skidded along the counter top.

Bannister scooped it up, hurling himself bodily away from the bar. He triggered, still in mid-air, the thunder making the lamp chandeliers jump, drowning the roar of the Colt. Something clipped his right shoulder, knocking him back against the bar front. Instinctively, he cocked the smoking gun again but he didn't need the second barrel.

Borden was down in a welter of blood, rammed into a corner by the charge of buckshot, head hanging, as if he was looking down at his mangled chest, examining the wound, wondering what had happened.

Bannister knelt, grabbed the man's hair and lifted the yellow-grey face and the fast-glazing eyes.

'You didn't give me Cordell's message.'

Borden was barely hanging on, but a touch of hatred gave a little life to his gaze, one final burst of energy.

'Longer you . . . live . . . better it'll . . . be,' he rasped, 'for Rance Cordell. Worse for you an' your wife an' kid . . . '

Blood gurgling up into Borden's throat caused a body-shaking, racking cough. When it was finished, so was Borden.

★ ★ ★

He left town by a trail that took him well away from Dander's Crossing, a pad on his shoulder over the slight bullet wound.

He was riding a big sorrel gelding with a searching eye that watched him warily: before he had felt the knife relieve him of his maleness, he must have been one helluva stallion, protecting his harem. But Manny Diego, the livery owner, had sworn the horse was 'accommodating' now.

'Justa take it nice an' steady, eh, Steve?' he suggested in his quaint accent. 'Get you to hell an' back you treat him the right, eh?'

'Manny, I've arranged for any insurance money to be sent to Ash Temple. He'll pass on what I owe you. I don't want anyone to know where I'm gonna finish up — fact, not even sure myself.'

'Issa OK, Steve. You gooda man with the hosses. You use him well, leave him somewhere wit' pipple he like — I trusta you to do that.'

'*Muchas gracias*, Manny. You and

other folk of Babylon have been mighty good to me. I've just had about the worst day ever in this town, but you and the others have given me a good feeling. Not likely we'll meet again, but I'll remember Babylon.'

He said *adios* and left town in the gathering darkness. He didn't care who was watching: he would change direction along the trail; later, not before midnight, cut through a high pass that would get him down to Dander's by sun-up . . .

Ash Temple hadn't been happy about the shooting in the Excelsior, of course, but Stacey and many of the drinkers swore Borden had gone for his gun first.

'My guess was he was pushed into it,' the hard sheriff said, sober-faced. 'You hit him first, I b'lieve, Steve.'

'Yeah. If I hadn't left my rifle with you I'd've shot the bastard where he stood — not killed him, 'cause I wanted to talk to him first — '

'Well, you got Cordell's message, so

now it's up to you when you quit town.'

Bannister smiled thinly. 'Left your tact at home today, I see, Ash.'

'I'm a lawman first, Steve, a friend second.'

'Yeah, well, I savvy I've stirred up the town like it's never been stirred in the five years since I came.'

'No. You've given us somethin' to remember, Steve — a real bad day in Babylon. You want, I can send Tatum to kind of ride shotgun; he'll hang back, out of sight, but he'll be there if you need him.'

'If I need him, Ash, it'll be too late for him to get to me in time. No, I know more or less what I'm going to do now.'

''More or less' don't sound quite good enough, not with someone like Cordell comin' after you.'

'I've some things in mind. That message he sent with Borden made me see what I have to do!'

They shook hands and Temple, for a moment, looked like he might apologize for playing it so hard, but in the end he just nodded. 'Good luck, Steve. You'll never pin anything on Cordell, you know. He's had a long time in jail and won't want to go back.'

'He won't be going back,' Bannister told him.

★   ★   ★

He cut away from the trail and was angling towards the difficult high pass through the range, when he heard the gunshots — behind him.

He reined in behind a stand of tall pines, sliding the rifle from the scabbard, levering a shell into the breech even as he swivelled in the saddle. The sorrel was behaving and stood waiting patiently, head turning as his nostrils twitched, scenting some grass. Experimentally, he took a step to one side, but Bannister's knees clamped tightly and he pulled the rein ends up and jammed them between his teeth.

The horse wasn't pleased but it obeyed.

Bannister lifted in the stirrups. There was a rider back there — the echoes of three shots fading already. *Three shots, evenly spaced:* the frontier call for help — *or attention.*

Which was it? Not that it mattered. He wasn't going back to investigate: they would know he wouldn't be that stupid, so what did the shots indicate?

He heard the horse then, racing in towards the foothills of the range, but angled some away from him.

'If you're looking for me, friend, you're way off-track.'

Then the voice called, 'It's Jack Tatum.'

The deputy was smart enough not to call Bannister's name just in case someone else was out searching for him, but he was sure he had left the town unobserved.

Bannister kicked the sorrel's flanks lightly, and it stepped out of the timber. He made no signal, just sat there in the open, rifle butt on his thigh, finger on the hammer-spur.

Tatum was a good outdoorsman, according to Ash Temple, and he would notice the faint difference in foreground colour of the stand of pines where Steve sat his mount. If he didn't, he might ride in circles all night, but Steve was not going to overtly give away his position.

Then he heard Tatum's horse starting up the slope: the deputy had spotted him.

'Don't shoot,' he called softly. 'Telegraph came for you. Ash sent me to give it to you.'

Bannister's belly knotted. It must be urgent for the sheriff to send out Tatum to find him.

It was — the message very short, and the worst news he'd ever had:

TESS MISSING. COME SOONEST,
IDA.

And that wrapped up his bad day in Babylon — with a real bang.

6

Bad Move

'Ash authorized me to ride along with you and help out, Steve.'

Bannister had recklessly lit a match so he could read the telegraph message and he shook it out now, but not before Tatum saw his head move side to side.

'Not necessary, Jack, thanks all the same.'

Bannister wheeled the edgy sorrel and touched him with the spurs. As the animal lunged away into the night, Tatum called, 'Ash *ordered* me to help you!'

'No!'

The refusal slapped back at the deputy and he swore as the drumbeat of the sorrel's hoofs diminished into the night. He lifted the reins and set his own mount after Bannister, but his horse was already tired from the hard, frantic ride out from Babylon with the message.

Swearing, he knew better than to whip a horse that had worked so hard and let it make its own pace.

Within minutes, he couldn't even hear the sorrel.

★   ★   ★

Bannister used his spurs on the rises and slopes, and once, to crash through a corner of a huge area of withers-high brush. The sorrel let him know he wasn't happy but obeyed and the rider had a sneaking suspicion the big gelding really enjoyed bulling its way through the brush, terrifying a lot of the smaller wildlife.

He glanced at the stars and figured he couldn't hope to reach Dander's Crossing before daybreak: he would have preferred to arrive in the dark. And if he took time to look for short-cuts, that time might be crucial to Tess's safety.

He hadn't given any thought about *how* she came to be missing: right now that wasn't important. Getting her back was, and just what that would entail was something else to think about.

But he had guns and fists, and know-how, and he would pit them all, and more, against whatever he came up against so long as Tess was returned safely to Linda.

And what about Linda . . . ?

Presumably she was still safe at Ida Farnham's or surely Ida would have mentioned something in the wire . . . or would she? Maybe she wouldn't want to worry him any more than that heart-stopping news about Tess.

So now that he had thought of it, heart-wrenching scenarios began to fill his head, clouding his brain when he most needed to keep his thinking crystal clear.

With an effort he pushed the panic-making thoughts aside: *Tess was missing!* Concentrate on that and don't make any mistakes that will delay arrival at Dander's!

He was disciplined enough to follow through on his decision and there was only a faint grey glow slightly tinged with deepening pink, in the east, when the lathered, hard-blowing sorrel came within sight of the ferry crossing.

The ferryman was barely awake when Bannister rang the bell at the landing, the clangour causing him to swear bitterly and start preparing his ropes and cables, and the harness for his quarter-horse team. His sidekick was stumbling about, half-dressed in patched overalls: both men seemed to get in each other's way but, at last, the big old platform with its sagging rails lumbered free of the other landing stage and began its jerky crossing, wet ropes rising out of the river as the pulley mechanism cut in.

Impatiently, Bannister waited, dismounted now, wetting a bandanna and wiping some of the foam from the gelding, its coat glistening.

The ferryman was heavily bearded

and had only one eye, the empty socket uncovered. He glared at Bannister.

'Been hazin' that mount some.'

'I'd like to haze you some, too — can we get moving?'

The older man spat into the coffee-coloured river. 'Always in a hurry, you young rannies.'

'With reason. My daughter's gone missing — she's only seven.'

'Hell! Why din' you say?'

He went to the bell in its weathered, crooked frame and clanged a series of signals that left Bannister's ears ringing. The man over the other side, stiffened noticeably, then slouched to the cable team and took a switch to them. The platform jerked under Bannister's feet and the sorrel snorted as it danced for firm footing.

'Obliged, friend.'

The one-eyed ferryman was staring hard at Bannister. 'I take it you don't want to wait for whoever's liftin' that dust way back yonder . . . ?'

Bannister didn't even turn to look,

just shook his head. 'You keep moving and you'll earn yourself a sawbuck.'

That obviously pleased the oldster who, just past the halfway mark, said, a little hesitantly, 'Was that you flankin' the Widder Farnham's surrey t'other night?'

'You got good sight in that one eye, old man.'

The ferryman hauled on the wet rope, Steve helping now, and it came hissing in, winding about the large pulley wheel. 'Can hear even better'n I can see. Like a feller asked me if a man with an ailin' wife and little blonde gal crossed on the ferry recently.'

Bannister locked his gaze on the old wrinkled face, showing more clearly now as the daylight strengthened. 'What feller was this?'

'Didn't know him, but he had a gold double-eagle to spend and — well, I . . .'

'You told him about my crossing with Ida Farnham?'

'I'm sorry, *amigo*, but it's been a long

time since I even seen a double eagle, let alone had one in my hands.'

Tight-lipped, Bannister nodded. 'Can't be helped.'

As the ferry nudged in to the landing on the far side, the one-eyed man said, 'He was a inch or two shorter'n you. Carried two Colts, cross-draw, wore leather chaps with lots of Mex conchos. Forkin' a bay with a black-tipped ear. Left one, I think . . . was mostly on my blind side.'

'Thanks, old-timer.' Bannister settled into leather after paying the man. 'Wouldn't happen to know where he went?'

'Said he was headin' north, but he rode west.'

Which didn't make a lot of sense, Bannister thought as he set the horse moving.

⋆   ⋆   ⋆

Ida was as distraught as Linda, likely more so, seeing as she claimed responsibility for losing Tess.

'She's a real little treasure, that gel,' she sniffed, awkwardly being comforted by Linda who moved stiffly with her ribs still strapped up firmly. 'Loved to collect the chicken eggs.'

She loved birds, Tess did, he thought not interrupting the widow.

'We got us a basketful and she wanted to go down to the duckpond, near our fence line, and look for more eggs. I explained that ducks don't lay as often as chickens, but she went skippin' off and — and — '

She couldn't hold back the sobs any longer and buried her face in her hands.

'Oh, don't, Ida! Please don't take on so. It wasn't your fault.' Linda's eyes were also tear-filled.

'It *was* my fault! I shouldn't've let her go so far from the house.'

Grim-faced, Bannister asked Linda, 'What happened?'

'She — she didn't come back in a reasonable time and Ida went looking and there was no sign of her.'

Steve frowned, putting an arm about

his wife's shoulders and squeezing, hoping it would comfort her at least a little. 'Any brush down that way? If she saw a bird fluttering about, she'd follow it to its nest.'

Ida was shaking her head emphatically. 'No brush that thick, just enough to screen North's fence from my kitchen window.'

'*North's?* That someone's name?'

Ida stopped sobbing and blinked, staring at Bannister, his tone both alarming and puzzling her.

'My neighbour — Asa North. He's only just put up that fence and Lord knows how, when only a week ago he said he couldn't afford to have his well hand-pump repaired and would have to go back to hauling with bucket and rope.'

'Does he have a feller, 'bout my size, wears leather chaps with conchos, workin' for him?'

'N-ooo, but I saw such a man talking to him. Asa works his spread alone — '

'Steve!' cried Linda. 'What — where're you going?'

'Headin' north,' he threw over his shoulder as he raced out the door.

The women, with their tear-wet faces, stared at each other blankly.

Asa North was a slim, short man but well-muscled. It was no effort at all for him to hold the long-barrelled Greener shotgun on Bannister as the big man hauled up his sorrel near the foot of the ranch-house steps.

'I've come for my daughter.'

'Will Sweeney's daughter, you mean, don't you?'

Bannister frowned, leaning his hands on the saddlehorn. 'My daughter — Tess Bannister. Seven years old and with long blonde hair.'

'Still Sweeney's kid. Her name's Bess not Tess. You changed it, I guess, when you took her from him.'

'The hell're you talking about, mister?'

'No! Don't bother gettin' down. You

ain't welcome here. Just turn that sorrel round and clear out back to where you come from ... an', I was you I wouldn't try to follow Sweeney. He knows how to use them guns he carries.'

Bannister settled slowly back into the saddle.' And how to throw double-eagles around, too, I bet.'

North frowned, his small face mostly in shadow now from the extra-wide brim of his hat. 'He's willin' to pay for information, if that's what you mean.'

'Yeah, that's what I mean. And you're willing to take his money. Look, North, I don't have time to listen. Sweeney's taking my little girl away from me further and further by the minute. Which way did he go?'

Bannister kneed the sorrel closer to the small porch and North's tongue flicked like a snake as he licked his lips. 'Don't you come no closer! Hell, I'd be in my rights to shoot you, trespassin', and a man who stole a child from its rightful parents!'

Bannister pushed up his hat and North took a hurried step backards as soon as his hand moved.' Did Sweeney tell you that?' At North's slow nod, Steve swore. 'What'd he say?'

'Well, his missus thought he was dead. He was missin' in a big fire up near the Muggy Own, lost his memory for a spell.' Bannister scoffed at this but North continued. 'She had a hard time tryin' to raise four kids, all buttons. Bess, the eldest, worked part time on a ranch to bring in a few extra cents. Cut a long story short, the rancher an' his wife took a shine to Bess and wanted to adopt her — paid cash-money to Sweeney's wife.' He paused and looked coldly at Bannister. 'You'd recall how much, I guess.'

'You think *I* stole Sweeney's daughter? Listen, North, I got no time to explain, but you believe this as gospel: *Tess* not *Bess* is *my* daughter! Mine and my wife, Linda's! And this Sweeney has you hornswoggled, seeing nothing but double eagles while he's taking her away from us! And if you don't put down that goddamned Greener I'll climb up there and take it from you, tie it in a knot around your neck and make you sit and watch while I burn down your goddamned ranch house!'

'Hey! You — you — ' North was backing-up: he had no intention of shooting and Bannister didn't waste any more time. He leapt from the saddle on to the porch, getting a shoulder under the shotgun's barrels and lifting them skyward.

The blast almost deafened him but the recoil made the weapon jump from North's grip and the man turned and dived for his door. Bannister reached out, caught him by the collar and dragged him back, shaking him, the cloth tightening about the small neck, the eyes bulging.

'You stupid son of a bitch! If Tess is harmed because of you delaying me — *Where did Sweeney go?*'

Half-choked, North gestured wildly, pointing over one shoulder towards the rising sun. In a rasping voice he said, 'Water-tanks — railroad. Gonna jump the freight to — to Tucson.'

'With Tess!' Bannister shook harder and North's short legs began to give way under him. 'When?'

'Due at tanks at — noon. You-you'll never make it.'

'If I don't, I'll be back . . . for you.'

Bannister flung the man off the porch, stepped over his floundering body in the yard and mounted the sorrel with a lithe movement, all weariness suddenly leaving him.

'Go tell the Widow Farnham, and my wife, what's happened — *you hear me?*'

North nodded shakily and Bannister wheeled the horse and spurred away towards the rising sun.

★ ★ ★

The big sorrel almost burst its heart but got him to the tanks just as the freight train was pulling away. The ground under the tank stand was dark and pooled with spilled water, more dripped from the nozzle of the canvas hose carelessly hooked to an upright.

A big bay horse, with a black smudge on the tip of the left ear stood in the shade, licking up some of the water from a shallow pool. It looked rested and fresh, compared to the jaded sorrel, with its dirt-plastered hide, caked with yellowish froth.

The train was a nine-car freight: actually, six were open wagons, a couple covered with tarps. There was the caboose and two box cars on the tag end.

As Bannister hauled rein on the now staggering sorrel, he saw movement in the caboose. The narrow sliding door this side was open and he glimpsed someone standing back from the edge, in the shadow. But sunlight flashed from several conchos where his legs would be: *Sweeney*.

Instinctively, Bannister unsheathed his rifle. The car started to sway as the train gathered speed, and Sweeney appeared again, this time holding Tess.

He held her with both hands in her armpits and she kicked and no doubt screamed as he dangled her in mid-air. Faintly, yet clearly, above the clatter of the train on the hot rails, the man's voice drifted through the stifling noon.

'Far enough, Bannister! We gotta cross that trestle bridge over Catamount Gorge a little ways up-track — hope your gal can swim!'

The message was plain enough: keep coming and Tess would be thrown off the train as it crossed the high trestle bridge over the roaring Catamount River, seventy feet below.

Bannister lowered the rifle: riding in openly this way, in his agitated hurry, he'd already made one bad move.

He couldn't afford another.

7

NO MERCY

The bay was friendly, happy, rested, with its thirst slaked. It nuzzled his shoulder as he came up and took its trailing reins.

There was no saddle in sight. So Sweeney had arrived early enough to remove it and take it with him when he boarded the train. No wonder the bay seemed refreshed, having rested for quite some time.

Bannister transferred his own sweat-dark saddle rig and, although the bay gave a token snort of displeasure at this sign it would be travelling again so soon, it stood still while he spoke quietly to it and adjusted the cinch strap.

He took time to rub down the big sorrel that was slurping at a pool now, washed off some of the caked foam and grit. He patted it as he tied the reins to a cross timber on the stand: it could still reach a small shallow pool but not the deeper ones where it might drink itself into trouble.

Someone waiting here for the next train through would find it. In any case, there was nothing else he could do.

He mounted the bay and rode off, testing it after a short distance with a touch of the spurs. The horse surged away beneath him and he patted its neck, raked the spurs a mite harder, and it began to stretch out in the first efforts of working up to a gallop. He only hoped it could keep up the pace and maybe more if he asked it to.

If he didn't catch the train and board it before it reached the bridge over the gorge, there was no way he could reach Tess.

★ ★ ★

He took a gamble.

From what he knew about cabooses

— and his knowledge was considerable, having ridden in dozens over the years with friendly guards happy to have some company on long rail journeys — they usually only had one sliding door and another swinging door, the latter in the rear wall, opening on to a small railed platform with a built-in gate.

The sliding door was always on the left-hand side, whichever way the train was travelling: the caboose hooked up so as to leave free access to the rear door and platform.

So, if he travelled on the *right-hand* side of the train, where the caboose wall was blank, except for two small, high-set windows, normally smeared and grimy, then he stood a chance of closing in without being seen.

But, if Sweeney was jumpy enough to look out one of those dusty windows, or stepped on to the railed platform —

No! It wasn't going to happen. It couldn't!

Tess was already in extreme danger so he had to take extreme chances. Not that such rationalizing made him feel any better. He was knotted-up inside like a greenhorn's lariat on his first round-up.

Bannister didn't know the country well, though he had passed through here before moving to Babylon. But he knew the railroad wound across the flats and into the foothills of the Buckeye Range, then passed through a cutting that had been blasted out of the solid rock, running slightly uphill. The cutting, together with the trestle bridge, saved many miles on the journey to Tucson.

What he was aiming to do, was to reach the cutting ahead of the train. There was enough of a hump in the grade through the hills to slow down the long freight train — and maybe give him a chance to swing on board.

Without Sweeney realizing it. That was the main thing. The Catamount Gorge was only a mile beyond the cutting. Once clear, the train would begin to gather speed on the downslope and —

He would have only minutes to rescue Tess.

*   *   *

The bay tried hard, willingly obeying his commands, putting in extra effort when he called for it. Judging by the old scars on the flanks, Steve figured Sweeney had conditioned the horse to instant obedience: no doubt the bay had gone through much pain and abuse before deciding it was better to give the rider what he wanted than to resist and suffer for it. It wasn't Bannister's way of training a mount, but for the moment he was grateful for the bay's quick responses.

The foothills loomed up and by now he had put a deal of side distance between himself and the train. Once he found a little cover given by sparse timber and brush, he had run the bay faster. Now he felt his heart almost skip a beat as he realized he was going to reach the cutting in time.

But only by a couple of minutes which would have to be long enough for him to hide the bay in the brush at the edge, grab his rifle and clamber into a position where he could drop on to the train.

Fatigue and lack of sleep were catching up with him, but during the wild ride he had decided to leap on to one of the tarp-covered wagons — and hope there wasn't machinery or something equally as hard underneath. Then he would make his way back to the caboose, find handholds and clamber on to the small platform at the rear door.

Then?

He was ready for those next dangerous few seconds of his entry, knowing the high risk of Tess being hurt if there was shooting, but, once again, there was no choice.

And he would sure show Sweeney no mercy.

★ ★ ★

The loco came into view above a tree-line, swaying as its belching smoke almost blotted out his view of the sky from where he crouched. He was hanging precariously on the rock wall of the cutting with one hand, rifle in the other. Now would have been the best time to pack a six-gun, but his Colt was at the bottom of his saddle-bags and there was no time to retrieve it.

In any case, he had his Big Henry rifle: fourteen cartridges in the magazine, one in the breech. If that wasn't enough — *hell, it had to be!*

No more time: he let go, thrusting away from the wall as the train swayed and clattered below him. He fell, twisting his body, trying to gain more distance from the cutting wall or he would fall between the freight car and the rocks and likely be mangled under the iron wheels. He lost his hat with the wind rushing past as he fell and then he slammed into the dirty, lumpy canvas.

The jar drove the breath from his body and he lost his grip on the rifle.

He slid on the rough tarp as he closed desperate, clutching fingers around the barrel, just below the foresight. Two more inches and he would have missed the gun altogether.

He lay there, gasping, body aching, something hard digging into his spine. He rolled to hands and knees, straightened, and worked the rifle barrel beneath his belt at the back, pushing it through almost as far as the breech. It tangled his legs, so he had to pull it up a few inches.

Between him and the caboose lay the two box cars, He would give his right arm for a rest but, glimpsing the trestle bridge drawing closer with every second, he forced himself forward across the canvas. The sides of the box cars had a narrow ledge top and bottom, but they were still in the cutting and, with the rocking of the train, he could see there was very real danger for a man clinging to the side.

So it had to be up and over. And, to his relief, he found a narrow iron ladder clamped to the end wall, leading up to the roof. His boots slipped on the narrow, worn rungs and once they thudded against the wall. *Lucky it wasn't the caboose where the sound would've alerted Sweeney!*

The car was rocking too wildly for him to attempt to stand up on the narrow plank walkway so he crawled along it, hands and knees rasped by splinters. It was a simple matter to slide across the gap to the next car's roof and crawl once more to its end.

The caboose was beyond and he slid over the shuddering gap, tearing one hand. He lost his grip and fell in the space between the cars, his good hand tightening around the edge of the box car. It hurt his shoulder wound which he had almost forgotten about until now, and for a moment thought he was going to fall. One glimpse of those rail ties whipping past below his boots was enough for him to find strength he didn't know he had. He pulled himself across, swinging his legs until a boot hooked the ladder. He clung there long enough to get a breath or two, then went up to the roof and sprawled on the narrow walkway.

He pulled himself across on his belly and without pause, dizzy from his exertions, swung down and dropped on to the small platform. Despite the ache in his muscles and his wrenched body, his reactions and co-ordination were still good. Even as he got the rifle clear of his belt, he kicked open the narrow door and went through, crouching.

His heightened senses gave him an almost panoramic view of the cramped inside of the caboose: the train guard sitting tensely on his built-in seat, hands clamped between his knees; Tess huddled at his feet, her small arms about the guard's lower legs for comfort. *There was a cut and bruise on her cheek, some dried blood at her nostrils, her upper lip swollen.* Rage surged through him as her eyes widened. Sweeney rounded in a blur of speed from where he had been standing at the partly open sliding door, watching the only side of the train he could see from here. One of his Colts whipped from his cross-draw holster, the motion very fast.

Bannister's rifle fired over the screaming Tess's head, fired again, hard on the heels of the first shot. Sweeney lurched, slammed back against the sliding door, one arm lifting over his head with the violence of the motion. He was still falling when Bannister took one long step across and used the smoking rifle barrel to slam the unfired Colt from the man's hand.

'*Daddeeee!*'

The child was clinging to him, thin arms about his waist, her head with the tangled, now dirty blonde tresses, pressed into him. He felt her small body start to rack with sobs of relief, stroked her head and murmured a few brief endearments, then said to the stunned guard, 'Look after her for a few minutes.'

The man nodded, still shocked by

the suddenness of the action that had erupted about him.

'Stay with the guard, honey,' Bannister told the crying child. 'I'll be back in a minute.'

He leaned down and grabbed the moaning Sweeney's shirt collar, dragging the man roughly to the open door leading to the balcony. Sweeney yelled in pain.

Bannister heaved him out on to the platform and closed the door behind him. He slammed Sweeney down into a corner, put the rifle on the floor and took Sweeney's second gun from his holster. The man was bleeding from two wounds, one low in his left side, the other in his right arm. His pain-filled eyes stared up at Bannister.

'Where the hell'd you come from?'

'All I want to hear from you is answers to my questions.' He cocked the Colt and Sweeney even managed a thin, though apprehensive smile.

'Kill me an' you won't know nothin' — '

'I don't aim to kill you; not yet anyway.'

Then Bannister yanked him to a half-sitting position, placed the gun muzzle beside the startled man's right ear and fired. The bullet whined away into space and Sweeney screamed. He clapped both hands over his suddenly bleeding ear, his skin grey, face contorted as he writhed. Slowly his bloody, shaking hand lowered and he said, 'You bust my ear drum! I-I can't hear!'

'I can, now this is what I want to know . . . '

They were just rolling on to the trestle bridge when Bannister had the answers he wanted — or as many as he could hope to get. Sweeney was a wreck, both ears bleeding now, head swaying loosely on his neck.

'I'm deaf!' he shouted, unable to hear his own slurred words.

Bannister said nothing, dragged the man to his feet and pushed him towards the low rail. Sweeney squirmed but was too weak to break Steve's grip. Seventy feet below them, white water roared and surged over jagged rocks.

'You wondered if Tess could swim a little while back — ah, hell! You can't even hear me, can you? Don't matter. Let's see if *you* can swim, you child-beatin' son of a bitch!'

Bannister shoved and released his hold on the screaming Sweeney at the same time, watching him fall.

Then he went back into the guard's quarters of the caboose and lifted the sobbing child into his arms.

8

VANISHING POINT

'Where in the name of hell *are* they?'

Rance Cordell stormed across the big parlour of his ranch house where several other men waited, most tensed, because they had seen Cordell in a rage before and knew he struck out blindly at anything — and anyone — within reach, with total lack of discrimination or repentance.

He looked not much better than the day Borden had met him at the gates of Yuma Penitentiary, though his clothes were neater, better quality. He had sent a wire to Tucson on his arrival at his ranch and ordered a tailor he knew there to '*haul your ass down here and bring or make me some decent clothes!*'

The tailor, Mr Rosen, came post-haste, bringing two assistants with armfuls of both ready-made clothes in varying sizes and bolts of cloth for Cordell's selection.

He decided he couldn't go through the ordeal of being measured by the fussy, effeminate old tailor and chose some shirts and trousers and a pair of boots, not his exact size.

That was when Mace McQueen, the Broken C ramrod — now thinking of himself as 'manager' — quipped, 'Should've had Bannister make you a pair before he disappeared.'

The room was silent, hardly a man breathing, as Cordell stopped his pacing and turned slowly to face McQueen. Without taking his eyes off the man, who looked a mite worried now, he told Rosen and his helpers to go back to town and he would pay when he was next in Tucson. Then he spoke very quietly.

'Mac, you did a fine job of caretakin' the ranch and I'm obliged. You even managed to find Bannister and hassle him some before I got outa Yuma

113

— *but you got a lousy sense of humour.* You take it down to the dam *right now* and see to the repair on those headgates.'

'Aw, Rance, I only — '

'*Right now! This very minute, goddamnit!*'

McQueen stood up from where he sat on the fat arm of an overstuffed chair, righted his hat and hurried from the room, face reddening. Cordell glared around.

'Anyone else want to audition for resident clown?' No one spoke, most not meeting his gaze. He nodded jerkily, mouth tight. 'All right, as I was sayin' — *where the hell has Bannister and his damn women gone!*'

Casey was the first to speak. He was on the payroll as a wrangler, but that was only as a sideline: he was one of Cordell's hardcases and had missed the usual 'special chores' and their associated 'bonus payments' while his boss had been in prison.

'We know he took the kid back across

the ferry to that widder's place, boss, after he took her off Sweeney. Far as we can tell, he only stayed overnight and' — he shrugged — 'well, next day all three was gone.'

Cordell's eyes blazed, focusing on Casey now, but the wrangler didn't seem fazed. 'Not just *gone*, but they've damn well *vanished*!' He raked his angry stare around at the others, most fiddling uncomfortably. 'You've all pulled down full pay all the time I was in Yuma! I come out and what do I get? Big glad welcome home, plenty of booze and grub, and everyone telling me they've got Bannister and his women on a plate. All I have to do is decide what I want to do with 'em.'

A thick-bodied man with a bald head and dark-green neckerchief, cleared his throat. 'Was Sweeney fouled up, boss, he should never've taken the kid. The deal was he was to watch the widder's place until Bannister showed, then we'd move in and grab all three of 'em. 'Stead, Bannister got word the kid was took and he went after Sweeney.'

'And caught up with the fool,' growled Cordell, thinking of the graphic description one of the men had given him of how they had found Sweeney's battered, barely recognizable body caught up in the rocks of the roaring river. The force of the water had ripped most of his clothes from his corpse and was starting to peel flesh from his bones.

'I think Sweeney had in mind to bring the kid here, boss, give you a chance to have Bannister come right to you, and then you could do what you wanted with him.' This was spoken by a slim, gun-hung man who looked dark enough to be a Mexican. His name was Shiloh and he had been Sweeney's sidekick on several past chores.

'Mebbe you're right,' Cordell conceded, surprising them all. 'But Bannister not only took his kid back and killed Sweeney while he was doin' it, now we don't know where the hell he is!'

'Could be that Babylon sheriff is helpin' him out,' suggested Casey.

'They was mighty friendly.'

'You want to go an' ask Temple?'

Casey pursed his lips. 'We-ell . . . '

'No! Only way we're gonna learn anything is go ask that widow — and Jack Tatum's still there.'

'I can take Tatum while I'm rollin' a cigarette,' said Shiloh confidently.

'Likely so — an' what the hell kind of hornets' nest you figure *that* would stir up? Ash Temple'd be down here in my front yard with a posse of a hundred men before you could spit! The US marshals from Tucson'd move in — and whether they could prove I had anythin' to do with it or not, I'd be back in Yuma: they'd find some violation of my parole conditions to put me away again. And *I ain't goin'* back!'

'Well, what do we do, boss?' Casey asked reasonably. 'We all want to see you square with this son of a bitch Bannister for gettin' you jailed, an' the best way of gettin' to him is through his family. I reckon we gotta get to this widder-woman somehow. Seems the logical place to start.'

'Tatum oughta know somethin',' chipped in Shiloh. 'Likely been helpin' Bannister all along.'

'Which brings us back to the problem of tanglin' with a sworn deputy in the course of doing his duty!' Cordell's voice was flat, his face tight with anger at the thought that after all this time, just after he was released, he might not yet be able to lay his hands on Steve Bannister and family.

Then he looked around the group one by one. 'Five hundred bucks to whoever finds Bannister — not just where he is, but *nails* the bastard and brings him back to me, complete with wife and kid!'

See if that would bring some results.

★ ★ ★

They knew they had to get their hands on Ida Farnham. Not only would she be easier to work on than Deputy Jack Tatum, but it was at least a ten-to-one shot that she knew *something* about where Bannister had taken his family.

Cordell was leery about harming Tatum: he knew how fragile was that parole. There must be a hundred people just waiting for him to put a foot wrong. He would just have to nudge a part of a toe over the line and the prison door would slam behind him for the remains of his sentence and he knew he could not face another fifteen years in Yuma.

So, when Shiloh had said heavily into a long silence in the ranch parlour, '*We need to get our hands on that damn widder-woman!*' Cordell instantly knew that was the only answer.

But Tatum was the problem . . .

All his men were eager to win that $500 in gold and a dozen suggestions were batted back and forth until Cordell himself came up with the solution.

It was so simple he felt like driving a fist through the wall for not having thought of it long ago.

What they had to do was separate Tatum and Ida.

* * *

Tatum was preparing to go back to Babylon.

He had stayed with Ida after Bannister and his family had gone, and knew Ash Temple would be champing at the bit now to have him back in town doing his normal chores. The sheriff had bent the rules a mite in order to help Bannister: it wasn't something the tough lawman would do for just anybody. But he and Steve seemed to hit it off pretty good and that was a rare enough thing for Temple.

Sometimes he was just too damn hard and refused to back off even a little. But he was into his mid-forties now and must realize he had no one to call a real friend, and a man needed friends, especially as the years built up.

Ida Farnham came out of the house with a calico flour bag bulging with goodies: corn dodgers, fresh biscuits, even an apple pie, which Tatum knew for sure would never reach Babylon in one piece. *He would see to that!*

'Tell Ash to come visit when he has time. Seems ages since he was out this way.'

'I'll tell him, ma'am, and thank you.' He slung the calico pack and prepared to mount. 'We'll keep an eye on you, but you'll be OK now the Bannisters have moved along.'

Ida frowned. 'Yes. I do wish Steve had said how we could get in touch, though. I'll miss both Linda and young Tess. Oooh, I'd like to've gotten my hands on that Sweeney, beating up on a child! It's disgraceful.'

'Bannister took care of Sweeney, ma'am.' Tatum didn't want the widow to get started on the subject. She had been sounding-off about Tess's abduction ever since Bannister had returned, enraged by her injuries which really weren't all that bad: kids were resilient, but it must have been terrifying for her

121

at the time, just the same.

Ida opened her mouth to speak, suddenly stiffened, pointing past Tatum's shoulder. 'We seem to have a visitor and in a hurry.'

Tatum turned, instinctively dropping a hand to gun butt. There was a rider coming in across the flats waving his hat wildly, shouting something the deputy couldn't make out.

'Know him?'

Ida shook her head. 'Hard to tell the way he's riding, but I don't think he's from around here.'

The man drew closer rapidly and they saw the sweat gleaming on his horse, dust settling on it as he hauled rein and the animal skidded to a halt.

'You the deputy?' he panted. He was dressed in worn range clothes, unshaven, red-eyed like any ranch hand who had been about his normal chores.

'I'm Jack Tatum. Who're you? And what's the hurry?'

'Cass Taylor — top hand at Broken C.'

'Cordell's place?' Tatum shook his head. 'Outa my jurisdiction, Taylor.'

'Hell! Pardon, ma'am.' Still panting from his ride he touched a hand briefly to his hatbrim. 'I-I can't ride all the way to Tucson! It'll be too late!'

'What's the trouble?' Tatum was tense now, frowning at Cass Taylor.

The cowboy waved vaguely behind him. 'We had rustlers last night. Traded some lead — two men were shot, including Mr Cordell.'

'I'll get some things together and come back with you,' Ida offered, and started to turn away but stopped at Taylor's clipped tones.

'No, ma'am! It — er — it ain't that bad. We've doctored 'em OK.' Taylor swung his gaze to Tatum. 'But you know Mr Cordell's on parole an' he's dead scared he'll do somethin' that'll violate his conditions and — '

'Wish he would,' muttered the deputy. 'What does he want? I can't do a lot officially, it not bein' my jurisdiction.'

'He's tryin' to do things by the book, Deputy. Can't blame him for that. He wants to report the trouble and have someone official like yourself take statements and so on. We heard you was here so he sent me to fetch you. You can come, can't you? He just wants it made official that the shootin' was none of his doin' and couldn't be avoided.'

Tatum sighed. 'Yeah, yeah, I can see how he'd want to avoid goin' back to Yuma. I can do it, but, truth is, Taylor, I don't give a damn. If I can put Cordell back behind bars, I'll be happy to do it.'

Ida placed a hand on his forearm. 'Now, Jack, you're a better lawman than that. No one's happy about Cordell running free, under strict conditions or not, but you have to be fair.'

'That ain't a word that Cordell knows, Ida.'

'I know, I know. But you're a better man than he'll ever be and you know the right thing to do.'

Tatum shuffled uncomfortably; he didn't need this widow-woman to stir his conscience. Reluctantly, he nodded. 'I guess so!' He muttered *Damnit!* as he turned to his horse and mounted.

'They're holdin' the ferry for us at the crossin', Deputy.'

'All right, all right! I'll stop by on my way back, Ida.'

'I'll be here.'

She watched them ride off, Taylor impatiently leading, turning in the saddle to urge Tatum on.

Smiling faintly, she walked back to the ranch house and went in through the kitchen door wiping her hands on her apron.

There was a man seated at the kitchen table, a dark man, like a Mexican. Shiloh smiled and his teeth were very white against his swarthy skin. He held up one of her biscuits he had been munching on.

'You a damn' fine cook, widderwoman. Come on in. My, ain't you nice-lookin' for your age! Hell, you shouldn't be without a man — '

Ida turned to run but another man

125

blocked her way and flung his arms about her, pinning her own arms to her sides. He grinned down into her face and she turned her head to avoid his sour breath.

'B'lieve we've met once or twice, ma'am, remember me? Casey, the Broken C wrangler . . . sometimes. Other times, well, lemme show you what I do other times, OK?'

As one rough hand groped at her clothing, Ida screamed.

But she knew it would do no good.

* * *

Tatum reined down when they came into sight of the ferry which was angled in to the river-bank on this side, pretty damn sloppily, he allowed silently.

He slowed his horse and swung towards Cass Taylor.

'Ol' Paddy musta been suckin' on the red-eye bottle when he nudged in like that.'

His words trailed off as he looked

126

into the muzzle of Taylor's Colt. The cowboy shook his head slowly.

'Me an' the boys ain't what you might call ferrymen, Deputy. Now you keep them hands folded on the saddlehorn. We got company, you want to turn your head a mite to the left an' check it out.'

Tatum snapped his head around and saw two more men holding guns on him, one a rifle, the other a sawn-off shotgun. 'The hell's this?'

'Aw, nothin' much — we just wanna have a talk with you.'

'Could've talked back at Widow Farnham's.'

'Well, couple other fellers were already booked to talk with her, but you an' me and my pards — we kinda like the idea of talkin' with you, just the four of us, huh?'

'By Christ, if that woman's harmed . . .'

Taylor smiled. 'What'll you do, Deputy? I gotta tell you now, you won't be able to do much — unless you can swim — but the river don't even go close by her spread, does it?'

The two men rode across and one leaned out of the saddle and removed Tatum's six-gun and rifle. He studied the men closely and one sneered and cuffed him, rocking him in leather. 'The hell you lookin' at, Tatum?'

'You boys're fools, messin' with an elected deputy — ain't the same as some gun-for-hire temporary man. I got laws backin' me and they make it mighty hard for anyone damn fool enough to try an' kill me.'

'We-ell, Mr Cordell knows that. Why you're gonna have an 'accident' an' be found floatin' face down in the river.' Casey's grin widened. 'After we finish our leetle talk, of course!'

Jack Tatum knew then he was a dead man: just openly mentioning Cordell's involvement was enough to ensure he wouldn't live beyond their questioning.

Thing was, he couldn't tell them anything: Bannister had refused to say where he was taking his family.

So, no matter what they did, he was

going to have to suffer, likely a helluva lot, too, all for nothing.

And poor Ida Farnham — she knew even less than he did.

He had nothing to lose. So he jammed his spurs savagely into his mount, rammed it into Cass Taylor's horse first, and the man reared in the saddle as the animal jumped and snorted and crashed into one of the others. The one holding the sawn-off, spun away to get free of the tangle. Tatum jumped his mount over Cass who was down and floundering, drove his startled horse head-first into the man.

There was another tangle of raking hoofs, wild whinnying and snorting. He jumped from the saddle, taking down the man with the shotgun. They hit heavily and the Broken C man was underneath. Tatum drove an elbow into his face for good measure, wrenched the gun around and, as Taylor and the other man ran in, fired.

The weapon jumped wildly in his

grip. Buckshot stopped Taylor and his companion in their tracks, both catching some, but not lethally. Trouble was, both barrels had fired at once, and now, as Tatum struggled to get to his feet he realized he was weaponless.

He flung the shotgun at the only man still mounted and the racing horse hit him and he went down under flailing hoofs. He grunted in pain as he rolled over and over, flopped into the edge of the river face down.

The Broken C ranny — Chico — instinctively and unthinkingly lifted his rifle and put two bullets into Deputy Jack Tatum's broad back.

'Judas priest!' groaned Cass Taylor, nursing a bleeding, though superficial, wound in his right side. 'That's torn it!'

9

Running

Tess Bannister did not like her new hair colour.

'But it looks all dirty, Daddy!' she said unhappily, fingering one of the 'sausages' that dangled about her head and which used to be golden.

'It's not dirty, honey, it's just dye. It's important that you — we all — look different now. We've got to try to fool Cordell's men.'

'Is that why you shaved your beard?'

'That's why. And why your mother had Ida cut her hair short and dyed it darker to match yours.'

Linda didn't particularly care for her own new hairstyle but the dark-brown colour didn't bother her much. She knew they had to do everything possible to throw Cordell's men off the trail.

Tess would come to realize it, too, eventually. That *mysterious* trail that would lead them who-knew-where. Because Steve Bannister wasn't saying. Ever since he had returned to Ida Farnham's with the frightened Tess, Linda had been asking him what they were going to do, where they were going. Her own injuries were healing fast now: she knew how fortunate she was that they weren't worse: there was nothing she could have done to prevent them. They could have killed her and the same applied to poor little Tess, helpess while that animal Sweeney — She stopped the thought hurriedly. Despite their present situation they had been very lucky so far. Yes, *lucky!*

Now she had to put all her trust in Steve and would do so willingly. But she still had reservations and an underlying fear that she knew would stay barely beneath the surface until — *until what?*

Cordell caught up with them? No! Steve wouldn't allow that to happen.

She was sure of that, but ... *always a 'but' when you lived on the edge of fear!* Cordell was such a powerful, unforgiving man. He had been humiliated, almost destroyed, by Bannister giving evidence that had cost him ten years in jail, and he would do anything to keep from going back.

He felt he had been disgraced before the world: men like Rance Cordell had feet of clay, no matter how tough they tried to appear. He would never be able to live with that until Bannister had been brought to heel, repaid in the only way his kind knew: he had to be killed, with all of his family. Show the world no one, *no one*, could defy Rance Cordell and hope to get away with it. And it had to be done in such a way that it could never be proved he had had anything to do with it. Let the law, let the whole damned world, *suspect*, even think they *knew* he was behind it, but it must never be laid at his feet officially. Even if he went bankrupt, he would ensure that. Money could buy anything. All it took was the right amount.

Bannister knew this and he had told Linda enough for her to use her own intelligence to see he was right.

Protecting his family was a tremendous responsibility, but she knew by now that Bannister had the strength and determination, and the know how, to carry it through.

She had full trust in him, but, at the same time, enough character of her own to mildly resent her own and Tess's dependence upon him. She knew it was foolish, but she couldn't put it aside entirely.

Linda Bannister didn't realize that it was just this trait of inner strength that enabled Steve to make the hard decisions, those he already had, and those still to come.

★ ★ ★

He took them west, but south of Sarhuarita, then slightly north until they came to the Indian Reservation known as San Xavier.

'You — you're not going to try to pass us for Indians?' Linda asked apprehensively, as she watched a band of half-naked braves sitting their saddleless mustangs twenty yards away, watching in silence. Two held rifles — old trade Lemans — another two had bows with arrows in buckskin quivers on their backs. The others had lances, the heads decorated with coloured feathers. *Wild* Indians, she decided.

Bannister smiled at Linda's question. 'Don't think I'm that good at disguises. No. I have a friend here, goes by the white man name of Buckets, don't ask me why, but his tribal name is Long Toes.'

She looked at him strangely and he frowned. 'What?'

'I just realized I don't really know you very well, Steve, even after being married to you all these years.'

He laughed. 'I did a short spell in the cavalry. Long Toes was our scout. I pulled him out of a river once. He was sure he was on his way to meet the Great Spirit, but he would've saved himself anyway.'

'And?'

He shrugged. 'Well, he figures he owes me something and he'll be happier if he finally gets a chance to repay me before he dies.'

She smiled slowly. 'Ah! Now I see.'

'Thought you would. Now let's go find him . . .'

It took some time and she listened in surprise as Bannister spoke to the Indians in their own language: she was learning more and more about her husband with every day that passed lately.

Long Toes had long white hair, braided, with totems and charms interwoven. His skin, though leathery, was remarkably smooth, but he must be at least fifty years old and most Indians of that age were heavily wrinkled. His buckskin headband was worked with all kinds of signs, some painted, some in Indian beads. He sat cross-legged in front of a traditional wickiup, before a small fire, the smoke of which he wafted towards him with an eagle's feather.

'Helps him commune with his ancestors,' Bannister explained in a low voice. 'He's a *shaman* now — kind of a medicine man — not a full-blown witch doctor, mostly heals people's ailments.'

'You have been long time coming, Naja.'

'But I have remembered you, Long Toes.'

'And I you, Naja.'

'*Naja?*' queried Linda.

'Kind of an open silver bracelet. I — er — happened to be wearing handcuffs when I pulled him from the river.' Her eyes widened, but he continued, switching to Indian, almost haltingly, with lots of sweeping and punctuating hand gestures. Obviously, it was a language he had to think about.

The old man listened, wafted more smoke, breathed it in deeply, finally looked hard at Tess, who clutched at her mother's upper arm, then at Linda and finally at Bannister. He nodded once.

'I must consider this, Naja. You will stay a short time.'

'It'll have to be short, Long Toes. My enemy has long arms and can reach almost anywhere in the land.'

'There must be preparations. And spells to protect you.'

Bannister sat back and Linda heard his breath as he released it in a slow sigh. 'He'll help.'

'How?'

Bannister hesitated, then said, succinctly, 'He'll chant a bit and blow smoke over us, then get us downriver to Nogales. After that, it's mostly up to us. But he has some contacts who'll kind of clear the way for us.'

'We're going to Mexico?'

He nodded, watching her face closely. 'You and Tess will have to learn a little more Spanish.'

'Because we'll be a Mexican mother and daughter? Is that your idea?' There was tension in her voice.

'No. Mexico's a hard place to pass as a Mexican if you're not one.'

She almost stamped her foot. 'Don't joke, Steve! This is a complete surprise! You've a right to treat my questions seriously.'

'Yes, I have — and I do. No, you won't be posing as Mexicans, but you'll be living amongst them for a short time.'

'I quite like Mexico although I haven't seen much of it. But what is your idea of a 'short time'?'

He stared soberly for so long she started to repeat the question, looking a little apprehensive. He forestalled her by raising a hand.

'I don't know, Linda, and that's the truth. I'm going to leave you with someone down near Magdalena — you'll be safe there. He has a large *rancho* and a lot of trustworthy men.'

Linda frowned. 'I'm not sure about this, Steve! Not just strangers, but someone who speaks a different language, lives differently . . . ?'

'It'll do no harm for Tess to see another way of life, and you'll enjoy it. Rafael will see to that.'

'Rafael? Our host, I take it?'

'Señor Rafael Santiago Ortega — with about a dozen other names somewhere in the middle, but they don't matter. He's an old-time *hidalgo*, Linda, and if your next question is 'How did I come to know him?' then I'll tell you. Briefly — when I was in the cavalry we were in a particularly hard action with Indians and some renegade white gun-runners. We were working with the Mexican Border Patrols. Anyway, my troop were with a Mex group under a young Capitan Jesus Ortega — Rafael's son. He was very eager, full of fire. He led his men in a charge between my troop, which was pinned down and being slowly slaughtered, and the renegades. It was one devil of a hand-to-hand fracas and in the end only seven of us were left standing. Unfortunately, Jesus wasn't one of them.'

He paused and Linda's eyes softened as she read the sadness in his face. *So like Steve to carry sad memories and relive them!* She placed a hand lightly on his arm but he didn't seem to notice — his mind was back in the bloody aftermath of that battle. Then he stirred himself.

'Our relief arrived just after it was all over but our captain had seen what Jesus did. He was mighty impressed. Told everyone who'd listen that Jesus was a hero and ought to have a medal. It took him weeks of lobbying headquarters, but in the end, the US Cavalry decided to award Jesus a Medal of Valour — There were politics in it, of course, but it was well meant, and I was given the job of delivering it to Rafael. It was kind of a rough journey down, through *bandido* country, and I had a couple of close calls. I was wounded before I reached Rafael's *rancho*. It impressed him that I'd come straight to him with the medal before getting medical attention — I never even thought of it, his *rancho* was closer than the town — anyway, he's been dying to do something for me in return.'

'And this is it? Asking him to protect Tess and myself? You seem to be calling in a lot of favours owed to you.'

She was surprised at the way his face straightened.

'It's not anything I'm proud of. Using friends.'

'Oh, Steve, I didn't mean to — '

He held up a hand and she stopped speaking. 'I've always been independent, Linda, as you've probably noticed.' She rolled her eyes but smiled to show she was only joking. He nodded and continued without smiling 'I don't consider either Long Toes or Rafael owe me anything. Long Toes would've gotten out of the river OK with a bit more effort, but I stopped, leaned down out of the saddle and hauled him across and took him to the bank without hardly thinking about it. I'd've done the same for anyone floundering in water that deep.'

'It must have given him a surprise. A

142

white cavalry trooper pausing to help an Indian.'

His glance sharpened. 'That's right smart of you, Linda, seeing it like that, because it's exactly the way Long Toes saw it. And, like most Indians, he'll never forget a good turn till the day he dies.'

'And this Rafael?'

'Same thing, really. I didn't figure I'd done anything much by taking him Jesus's medal: I just figured he'd like to have it. I don't like calling in this favour, but I can't think of any other way. Aw, he'll be glad to do it, and at least I'll know you'll be safe.'

'While you do what?'

He took a short time to answer, said quietly, 'Something I should've done a long time ago: go and do the world a favour by killing Rance Cordell.'

★ ★ ★

Sheriff Ash Temple thumbed his hat back, used his sleeve to blot up the sweat on his forehead. As he lowered his arm, he looked again at Ida Farnham's abused body, sprawled on the floor of her disarrayed bedroom.

He glanced away again almost immediately. *Goddamn! If ever he caught up with the scum who could do this to a decent human being like Ida!*

He knew who it had to be: knew just as surely that he would never be able to prove it. As soon as the word had reached him about Ida, and that Jack Tatum was nowhere to be found, he hired two temporary deputies, McGregor and Kinloch. The trio had ridden out here as fast as they could.

Doc Penney had followed and was now sitting in the kitchen, his cup of coffee growing cold, staring listlessly at the floor. He had loved his sister, blamed himself for having involved her in this. *Damn Steve Bannister!* Still, he had to be fair: Steve's family had already suffered. It had seemed the right thing to do to offer them some sort of sanctuary with Ida. Now it had cost his only sister her life.

The sheriff called to Bill McGregor and they lifted Ida's near naked, blood-streaked body on to the bed. Ash pulled a bloodstained sheet across her.

McGregor, a young townsman who lived with his mother in Babylon, had turned white, now hurried from the room.

Down in the yard, the other deputy, Ramsay Kinloch, straightened from trying to decipher the mess of hoof-prints as McGregor burst out the door and threw-up in Ida's flower bed. Kinloch was a tough bronc-buster who freelanced around the counties, and happened to be between jobs when Temple had hired him. His eyes narrowed at McGregor's reaction.

'Dunno as we're gonna find the bastards, Bill, sorry to say — take an Injun to unravel these tracks. There're more down by the gate.'

'Well, go check 'em an' compare!' McGregor snapped, wiping his mouth, a sob at the edge of his voice. 'She — my ma's about the same age as Ida was!'

Kinloch nodded, genuinely sympathetic. 'Don't reckon we'll be takin' prisoners if we do catch up with 'em.'

He moved away and was kneeling by the prints down by the frame gate when Ash Temple came out of the house. At the sheriff's quizzical look, Kinloch shook his head.

'They've drug somethin' over the tracks to mess 'em up.' Then he stopped, flicking a gaze towards McGregor. *The 'something' must have been Ida, at the end of a rope.* 'None of the tracks I can make out leads towards Babylon.'

'We better check the river; they might've crossed it.'

★ ★ ★

The older ferryman, Paddy, was dead, but his assistant, Jed Walden, was still alive, though wounded. Temple sent McGregor back to fetch Doc Penney from Ida's — tending Walden would give the medic something to do apart from grieving for his sister.

146

Jed had a bloody wound in his chest and half an ear missing on the right side, painful wounds but not fatal. While examining them, Temple asked what had happened.

'Guess they figured I was dead an' rode off.'

Ash tried to contain his impatience. 'Who, dammit, Jed? Who did this? And where's Jack Tatum?'

Jed gestured wearily to the wide river. 'Carried away on the . . . current . . . after they shot him.'

Kinloch swore and the sheriff's lips compressed.

'*Who*, for Chris'sakes?'

'Dunno for sure. Could've been Cass Taylor. Hoss was branded Broken C, but they don't use this ferry, do most of their business in Benson, bein' closer, so I ain't sure.'

'Broken C — Rance Cordell.'

Jed jumped, maybe because Kinloch was washing the wound in his side while they awaited Doc Penney, and touched a tender spot, or maybe because Cordell's name had been mentioned. He licked his lips and said quickly, 'Couldn't swear any of Broken C rannies was here, Ash. I . . . wouldn't wanta get nobody into . . . trouble.'

Temple's lips thinned out. 'Mostly yourself, I s'pect! Wonder you even mentioned Tatum bein' shot!'

Jed closed his eyes and his voice was whining as he said, 'Gawd! I'm hurtin' . . . I couldn't do nothin' to help Jack or Paddy . . . gospel, Ash.'

Temple nodded wearily. 'No use askin' you why Tatum was here, I s'pose?'

Jed shook his head. 'Couldn't hear 'em talkin'. I was on t'other side.' He gestured weakly across the wide river. 'I-I think mebbe they decoyed him away from that widder's place so they could get to her.'

That was it, all right, Temple silently agreed.

'What do we do next, Ash? Go see Cordell?'

Temple stared long and hard, but Kinloch returned his gaze unwaveringly.

'Outa our jurisdiction, that side of the river. Not even worth notifyin' the Benson sheriff: no one'll find anything to prove Cordell sent men over here.' He shook his head in frustration, then turned to Jed, who was groaning now as Kinloch wrapped a rag around to cover the mutilated ear.

'Unless your memory's suddenly improved?'

Jed lowered his gaze, shook his head.

'They got us hogtied,' the sheriff said disgustedly.

'Well, hell, Ash! We gotta do somethin'!'

'That we have, Ramsay. We got three dead people, includin' Jack Tatum. And the other thing is, the Bannisters are missing. Were they taken by Cordell's men? Or did they get away before anyone arrived? Help us out here, Jed.'

'Can't. Steve Bannister never showed up here, but he could've crossed the river at the ford upstream. Some folk do, to save payin' ten cents on the ferry.'

Kinloch said, 'You're Steve's friend, Ash, din' he tell you what he had in mind?'

'No. Said it was better if no one knew where he was taking his family, and I had to agree. It made sense.'

'Not right now it don't.'

'No, Goddammit! If he told Ida his plans and those bastards broke her . . . ' The lawman shook his head angrily. 'Well, Steve's gonna have one helluva time of it. And that includes Linda and the girl, Tess.'

'And ain't a blamed thing we can do!' Kinloch's cussing in his frustration was blistering.

Temple kicked futilely at the ferry platform. He glared at the wounded Jed, but the ferryman wouldn't look at him. 'Doc'll be here soon. Ramsay, get the mounts: we're goin' downstream. With a little luck we might at least recover Jack's body.'

'Then what?'

'Good question — *damned* good question.'

10

Magdalena Trail

They gave the horses to Long Toes.

The old man had decided that the best and safest way to reach Nogales was for the Bannisters to use the Santa Cruz River. Groups of Indians travelling by canoes and rafts were quite common on the river, taking goods down to Nogales to trade with the Mexicans. There were family groups, as well as hard-faced warriors, the latter usually looking for guns.

'They'll give you both buckskin dresses and stick a feather in a headband,' Steve explained to an apprehensive Linda and Tess. 'Would've been better to have left your hair long, as it turns out, but Long Toes has got a couple of his squaws making you horsehair braids to attach so you'll look like Indians.'

'That won't pass close inspection!' Linda said.

'Not meant to. It's for anyone watching from the banks as the canoes go by. Just stay low, but you'll be expected to take a turn at paddling.'

Linda looked at him calmly. 'At least it'll be a new experience.'

He smiled, ruffled Tess's hair. 'You'll have plenty to tell your friends.'

Tess pouted. 'If I ever see them again.'

Bannister's smile faded a little: it was true. They probably would never return to Babylon: it was good that Tess realized the possibility. He hoped that, in time, she would come to accept that they had now cut all ties with their past life, might even have to change their name: it was all up to him.

He had to go after Cordell and beat him. And there was only one way to do that: *kill the man*.

Long Toes was grateful for the horses to add to his already large herd: he was happy that he was able to help

Bannister after all these years.

Linda asked Steve suddenly, when they were helping load the canoes and a small raft that would be carrying some of the bulkier items for trading, 'How come you were wearing handcuffs when you rescued Long Toes from the river?'

'Didn't really rescue him, only helped him a little — but, no big deal. It was before the battle where Jesus Ortega saved my troop. We were passing through badmen's territory and knew there was a gang that'd been dodging us for a long time. We hardly spotted anyone as we searched; they'd go under cover soon as someone reported cavalry riding close by. The captain came up with the idea of one of us infiltrating the gangs and I drew the short straw.'

'What does that mean?'

'I was to act the part of a prisoner. My story was that I'd attacked an officer and was heading for a firing squad back at the fort, so I'd be seen as a pretty desperate character, hand-cuffed and all.'

'It sounds dangerous. Did it work?'

'Well, I made my *escape*, still wearing the cuffs, and the troop made a big show of shooting at me and trying to hunt me down. I saw Long Toes in trouble and dragged him out of the river, then rode on and later was picked up by an outlaw group. They believed my story and accepted me into the gang, but the men we wanted had already gotten away into Mexico. So it was all for nothing.'

'What did you do?'

'Waited for an opportunity and broke away, rejoined my troop about a week before the big battle where Jesus saved our hides.'

Linda's eyes travelled over his face and she smiled slowly. 'You are a secretive man, Steve Bannister! Until now, I didn't even know you'd been in the cavalry.'

He grinned and squeezed her shoulder. 'Man of mystery, that's me.'

She nodded, sober now. 'Yes — the lone wolf. You don't let people get too

154

close, do you, Steve?'

'Only you and Tess. When this is all over, I'll tell you my life story, if you like: unabridged.'

'I'll believe that when it happens!'

It was a picturesque river journey and Tess grew quite excited on some sections where there were rapids and white water, squealing in delight as she clung to the side of the canoe, drenched in spray. Linda was more reserved and tense but slowly relaxed as the miles slipped by. Both went part of the way on the raft, staying out of sight inside the small *tipi* on board, but Bannister stayed with the canoes.

They timed the arrival in Nogales for sundown, set up camp outside of the town. While the Indians began bargaining right away with the traders, both Mexican and Anglo, the Bannisters dressed in their normal clothing and were taken across into Mexico where a band of Apaches were waiting. They knew all about the Bannisters and their destination.

'How is that possible?' Linda asked, genuinely perplexed.

'Don't ask me. Told you Long Toes is a *shaman*. He claims he can contact people over huge distances with what he calls 'mind messages'. That's all I know. I've seen it before and whatever they do, it works — for which we should be mighty grateful.'

The Apaches said little, mostly communicated by signs, and led them south.

'Is this the trail to Magdalena?' Linda asked, as they climbed mountains, wound their way through narrow passes where they had to ride single file. 'It's awfully rough.'

'It's the Apache's special trail: they do a lot of business with the Mexicans. The regular trail is some way to the east, I think. Long time since I've been down this way.'

'As long as they know what they're doing.'

They did. A few days later the Apaches led them out of a winding, broken path through low hills and the leader pointed ahead.

In the distance was a white-painted building on a rise, with the green of trees and some grass surrounding it. Beyond were herds of cattle and moving dots which were riders going about their chores.

'Ortega,' the Apache said, wheeled his mount and rode off, the other Indians following.

'They're not even waiting for a thanks.'

'It'd mean nothing to them. They're wild Apaches, part of the Sierra Madre group, been dodging the army for years. Normally, they kill white men using the Magdalena Trail.'

Tess grimaced and looked sharply at her mother whose eyes had widened.

'My God! And we were travelling with them for days!'

'We were safe. Long Toes has arranged it all. We'd be safe if we wanted to turn round and go back, too, but I don't know how much longer his protection will last.'

'Or if we'll ever be going back north again.'

Bannister just gestured towards the *rancho*.

'Let's go meet Don Rafael.'

*   *   *

Rafael Ortega was a gentleman, courteous in the old style, attentive to both Linda and Tess. But his eyes could harden when he was giving orders to his *vaqueros*, or if a man had not done his work properly. This was merely on the surface, of course, the verbal disciplining of a subordinate: the real punishment and Rafael's displeasure would be expressed more explicitly down at the bunkhouse later, away from the eyes and ears of his guests.

'Señora Bannister, it gives me the greatest of pleasure to be able to assist you in any way I can.' He was a short man, thickening about the middle, but still retained handsome facial features.

His teeth flashed white, surrounded by grey-streaked pointed beard and trimmed moustache. He raised a glass of wine. 'I am indebted to your 'usband.'

He gestured towards a heavy mahogany cupboard on which, standing alone on a narrow shelf traversing its length, was a gilt frame, displaying a medal with coloured ribbons under glass.

'My only son's Medal of Valour. No one can know just how much this means to me. And I say to you all, whatever you wish and it is within my power to provide, it is yours.' He smiled a little wider in Tess's direction and winked. 'I naturally, include you, *querida*!'

Tess seemed a little flustered but smiled and as the others drank their toast in wine, she sipped her sweet lemon syrup.

'I like that little grey foal in your small corral, Señor Ortega,' she said, with a quick flick of her eyes towards her parents. 'Could I ride it, d'you think?'

'Tess!' Linda said sharply and Bannister frowned at the child, shook his head slightly.

Ortega laughed. 'It is yours for as long as you wish. When — if — you leave, the foal can go with you.'

'Now listen, Don Rafael — ' began Bannister, but the *ranchero* held up a hand.

'It is done, Steven. And you, Señora Linda? You have something I can give?'

'Not right now, thank you, Don Rafael.' She threw a quick frown in Tess's direction, but the happy child feigned not to see her mother's disapproval of her temerity.

Later, well after the meal was over and Linda and Tess had retired, Ortega handed Bannister a cut crystal glass of brandy to go with the thick cigar Steve was smoking.

'Your plans, Steven. How can I help?'

'Well, I have a rough idea of what I'll be doing, Don Rafael, but no details. I won't be able to fill them in until I get back to Cordell's country and see for myself just how he has set himself up. I assume he'll be heavily protected.'

'You are going to confront this man?' Ortega frowned a little. 'I know his reputation — or as it was before he went to prison. He is a most dangerous man. And has many dangerous men working for him.'

'I know, but I think I can dodge 'em. A lone man can be harder to run down than a whole bunch of riders.'

'Riders or raiders? I think perhaps the latter term is more suitable!'

'Make it *raider* and you'll be pretty close.'

Ortega paced the carpeted floor in front of a huge portrait of a galleon on the high seas, sails stretched taut in a following wind, the crimson cross of Spain curving against the weathered canvas.

'I have men I trust implicitly who could ride with you, Steven. You will need some protection, too.'

'No, thanks, Don Rafael. I appreciate the offer, but this is something I have to do alone.'

'*El lobo solo*, as your beautiful wife called you, eh? Ah, I understand, Steven. You are a *bravo* as I once was, like my ancestors, the *conquistadors*. But this is a terrible man you have chosen for your *mano a mano, amigo*: it will be a fight to the death.'

Bannister sipped brandy and looked over the glistening rim of the glass at Ortega.

'You said it, Don Rafael. The only way this thing can be resolved is by a fight to the death.'

The Mexican met his gaze and held it. He nodded gently, raising his glass slightly.

'Then — to your victory, *mi amigo*.'

They drank silently.

11

Arrival

Sheriff Ash Temple sat on the log, packing his pipe, but, when the bowl was full he made no attempt to light up.

Instead, he leaned his forearms on his thighs and stared down the slope of coarse sand to where the river lapped it in this small inlet. A man lay face down and unmoving, upper body on the sand, boots trailing in the water. One leg moved slightly with the weak current, but the lawman's gaze settled on the torn, sodden shirt and the two bullet holes under the left shoulder.

Jack Tatum's hat was missing, his tousled hair filled with sand. There was a pale, jagged cut where his temple had come into contact with a rock while floating down the river from the ferry crossing.

Ramsay Kinloch took a blanket from his bedroll so they could wrap the body in it. He sat down next to the sheriff, the blanket trailing on the ground.

'We could do with another horse to carry him, Ash.'

'Known Jack a long time. Good deputy. Would've made a damn good sheriff.' Temple ignored the mention of a horse to take the corpse into Babylon.

'His wife's carryin' again, you know.'

Temple's head snapped up. 'Pregnant?' At Kinloch's solemn nod, the sheriff swore, and lit his pipe, using three matches before he was satisfied with the way it was drawing. He looked through the blue smoke at Kinloch.

'Ramsay, you ride to Ida's place with Jack. Then you and Bill go back to Babylon with Doc. He can take Ida and Jack in the buckboard: he'll want to lay her to rest where he can visit. You'll have to see Jack's wife.'

Tight-lipped, Kinloch nodded unhappily, then asked, 'Where you goin'?'

Ash Temple removed his badge from

164

his shirt pocket.

'I'm outa my bailiwick over the river, but that don't mean I can't still hunt down a murderin' snake like Rance Cordell as an ordinary citizen.' He held out the badge towards the deputy whose jaw dropped. 'Makin' you temporary sheriff of Babylon, Ramsay. If I don't come back, you're permanent. The town council'll back you. You got a good rep.'

Ramsay Kinloch blew out his cheeks. 'Hell, Ash, that's kinda risky, ain't it? I mean, you nail Cordell without your badge to back you and they'll throw the book at you.'

'Won't matter, will it? The bastard'll be dead.'

'Judas priest! Well, what about Bannister?'

'I don't really know what he's doin'. Mostly he wants to hide out his family. Protectin' them is his first priority, which I can savvy.'

'Uh-huh. But Steve's a tough man under that quiet saddler look we all

165

knew these past five years, Ash. Wouldn't surprise me none if he stashes Linda and Tess, then goes after Cordell.'

The sheriff's face was set in hard lines as he nodded slowly. 'My notion, too, and if he gets there first, I guess that'll be fine with me. But I can't just ride away from this with Jack Tatum lyin' dead at my feet, back-shot into the bargain: someone has to pay for that. You gonna take this badge or do I throw it in the river?'

Kinloch pulled at his lower lip, then slowly held out his hand. He closed his fingers over the well-used brass star.

'I admire what you're doin, Ash, but it ain't like you. Bendin' the rules, even for a friend like Bannister. This time you'll be *breakin'* 'em. Anyways, I sure as hell hope you come back and pin this badge on your own shirt again.'

'Well, if I do, you'll know Cordell's dead for sure, whether it was me got him or Steve. If I don't show up in a reasonable time, you contact the US marshals, tell 'em everything that's happened. I know the Chief Marshal, Miles Parminter, and he'll find some way of getting that son of a bitch back behind bars. It's second best, but better than lettin' Cordell run loose.'

★ ★ ★

'Hell almighty!' Rance Cordell gritted, almost flinging himself over the big ranch-office desk as he lunged to his feet. The four men standing on the carpet in front of the desk hurriedly took a step back when they saw his face.

His murderous eyes were set on the cowboy standing between Cass Taylor and Mace McQueen. It was Chico, the wall-eyed ranny about thirty, unshaven and dishevelled from long trails — and from twice trying to make a run for it when returning with the others from the ferry.

'You're gonna face Rance over this, Chico,' Taylor had told him coldly after he was brought back. 'You done it, an' now you can explain to Rance. You try to run again and I'll shoot you through both feet.'

That had put a stop to Chico's escape attempts.

Now the man swallowed, his Adam's apple rising and falling swiftly. 'I figured he was gonna get away, Mr Cordell,' he whined, rubbing his hands together. 'I just never thought about it, wanted to stop him so I shot him.'

'You're right about one thing, Chico, you never *thought*! My orders were Tatum wasn't to be shot! He was to meet with some kind of fatal accident that could never be traced to Broken C!'

Cass Taylor cleared his throat and inwardly winced as Cordell swung his bleak stare towards him. 'He'd've floated a long way in that current, boss. He'll wash up pretty damn far from here. No one'll know we had anythin' to do with it. I mean, the widder won't be talkin', will she? Both the ferrymen are dead. No one'll be able to connect us to any of it.'

Cordell merely swivelled his gaze back to the shaking Chico. 'You can't obey orders, I got no use for you. Take him out.' His eyes narrowed now as he looked again at Taylor. He didn't have to add anything else: the look and the tone of voice told Taylor what had to be done.

He turned his hat between his fingers and nodded curtly: no use arguing.

When Chico had gone, yelling for mercy, McQueen poured two drinks at a polished sideboy and handed a glass to Cordell.

'I think it'll be OK, Rance. Temple's got no jurisdiction this far from the river anyway, even if he tries to involve us.'

'You're getting as stupid as the rest of 'em, Mac. Temple'll come, make no mistake about it. He might not be able to prove anything about Tatum, but he can stir up trouble for me with that damn parole board.'

'Hell, Rance, you got 'em in your pocket! They been paid plenty!'

'Damn right, and if they see another way to prise a lot more dollars out of me, they'll do it. I don't pay up, they simply decide I've breached my parole conditions and I'm back inside Yuma!'

McQueen had learned long ago not to argue with Cordell when he was in one of these moods — and possibly only McQueen knew why: Rance Cordell was scared witless of Steve Bannister, though you would never get him to admit it.

One man, badly misjudged by Cordell and his backers . . . *just one man!*

And, as if to confirm the ramrod's thoughts, Cordell tossed down his drink and thrust the empty glass towards McQueen.

'Fill it to the brim this time, *and find out where the hell Bannister is!* I don't want to step out on to the porch some morning and find him sitting at my breakfast table! Goddammit! Will you hurry up with that drink?'

McQueen handed the brimming glass to the rancher who spilled some of the golden whiskey on his hand as it shook while he lifted it to his mouth.

Annoyed at this display of how rattled he was, he turned and hurled the crystal glass into the fireplace where it shattered, the shards glinting in the light of the oil lamp on the desk.

Cordell glared challengingly at McQueen, but the ramrod remained cool.

'It's been three days, Rance. Temple should've showed up here by now if he was comin' at all. He might not've been able to leave Babylon right away.'

'I don't need you thinkin' up excuses, figuring it'll make me feel good! And Ash Temple isn't the top of my list.'

McQueen sipped his own drink. 'I doubt Bannister would be close enough to have arrived here yet and he'd have to get by the men I've got ridin' the fences and watchin' every trail in here. We can handle Bannister, Rance. Hell, might be best if he does show up! Then we can kill the son of a bitch and you'll know he's outa your hair for keeps.'

The rancher stared coldly, then nodded gently. 'Yeah, but it's not ideal! That bastard's put me through the worst hell of my life — I want him to suffer plenty first. And the best way to do that is get his wife and kid and make him watch when I turn the boys loose on 'em!'

Yeah, that'd be your style.

'I've got a couple of the boys spreading some money around along the border. That might produce somethin'.'

It didn't seem to make Cordell feel any better.

* * *

At that moment, Steve Bannister was slipping a belt of cartidges over his head and across his chest. Every loop was filled. The Henry's tubular magazine was also full and there was an extra shell already in the breech.

He was ready for war.

Don Rafael had given him a sleek-bodied brown horse with a good deal of Arab in his lines. It had to be worth a lot of money but the old *ranchero* had insisted. He had tried to talk Steve into taking one of the latest Winchester rifles he had a small stock of — 'For the use of my friends, naturally,' the Mexican had said with a crooked smile: his 'friends' included, of course, the revolutionaries he was quietly backing.

'These rifles are very good, Steven. They are made to fine tolerances, with flip-up peep sights on the stock. I have some specially hand-loaded cartridges and with your already fine marksmanship, you will find your target.'

'No thanks, Don Rafael. It's a fine piece of gunmaking, but I'm used to the old Henry, can almost make it sit up and beg. I know just what it can do, what ranges are best, how far it will shoot and still be effective. I don't have the the time to work with a new gun.'

'You still do not carry a six-gun — ?'

'Got one in my saddle-bags. A

cavalry trooper mostly shoots a rifle and while a single-shot Trapdoor Springfield — normal issue — makes you learn to hit your target every time, I like the Henry with fourteen shots, fifteen with one in the breech after the magazine's full. The six-gun has always been a trooper's back-up, but if I can't get my man with fifteen shots . . . ' He shrugged.

So he rode north for the border with a group of Ortega's vaqueros, even wearing a fancy waistcoat and sombrero. This way he was not only protected on his long ride, but it made it mighty hard to identify him amongst the Mexicans. And he didn't aim to underestimate Cordell: he would have men watching the border and the country around Broken C.

The group, under Ortega's *segundo*, Monte Pasar, were ostensibly looking for longhorns to introduce into Ortega's herds and so would be riding through border country until they reached a place where Bannister could safely leave them and carry on alone.

Which suited him. He was mighty grateful for Ortega's thoughtfulness in offering him that group of *vaqueros* to give him cover on the long ride up from Magdalena. Getting from Magdalena to the border had been one of the problems that had worried him before leaving. It had worried Linda, too.

'It's such a long way, Steve! And a lone *Americano* riding north through this country will attract attention.'

That had been his main worry, until Don Rafael had solved the problem: even Linda had been relieved.

And he knew she and Tess were safe now, whatever happened to him . . .

⋆   ⋆   ⋆

He left the vaqueros the day after they arrived back in border-country USA. They left Cananea, south of the Rio, crossed on a line with Bisbee. Here they let it be known that Don Rafael Ortega of Magdalena was looking for top quality longhorns for a breeding experiment with his imported herds.

Ortega had done business with the southern Arizona ranchers before and offers came in from the surrounding spreads. Pasar divided his men into small groups of two or three to go and inspect the cattle. He kept Bannister with him as they rode towards a ranch north-west of Bisbee in a dusty basin called Pancake.

'Here is good place to say adios, *amigo*,' Pasar said.

When the ranch was in sight, still far off, Bannister took his leave, shedding the sombrero and waistcoat, shook hands with the *segundo* and disappeared into the heat-haze.

Two days later, having dodged obvious patrols of riders watching out for him, he crouched amongst the shadows of a stand of timber halfway up the slope of Broken C's home range.

He not only had a good view of the ranch and its inner pastures, but could see some of the outlying ones, and had found a shallow cave with a broken line of fallen rocks across the entrance. It was a good hiding place and could be defended well if necessary. He had a bag of oats for the Arab, named *Flecha* by Ortega — 'Arrow' — and there were small patches of grass not far downslope where he could let the horse feed after dark. To make it perfect, there was a dribble of water from rainwater held by the limestone above and slowly filtering through. It was a mere trickle but constant and a saddle canteen would fill overnight. He planned to leave the spare canteen there by day so it would be filled when he returned from —

Whatever hell he could think up and perpetrate!

He had decided Cordell not only needed killing, but because of his ruthlessness and murderous intentions towards himself and his family, that the man should be made to suffer first.

This did not mean capturing the rancher and submitting him to sadistic torture; there were other ways that could hit Cordell mighty hard, shake him up, working him up to perpetual fear, never sure where Steve would strike next.

What he had to do now was figure out just what would drive Rance Cordell to the brink of insanity and, when the man was broken, a red-eyed, near-gibbering wreck, *then* Bannister would deliver the killing blow.

Rough justice, perhaps, but the only kind for a snake like Cordell who could buy his way out of the legal system over and over.

Strip him of his money and his means of making it, and he would be at Bannister's mercy.

Of which he had absolutely none where Rance Cordell was concerned.

Mess with Bannister and he would accept that, fight back hard, *really* hard, but mess with his family and whoever was stupid enough to try it had better start picking out the epitaph they wanted on their tombstone.

12

Shadow Man

The one they called Shiloh was riding alone, checking the waterholes for fresh tracks, in case Bannister had already slipped through the net.

He found nothing, dismounted and sat beneath a tree and rolled a cigarette. He lit up, closed his eyes, legs drawn up, one arm resting on his right knee.

Damn he was tired! The boss must be mighty rattled, the way he divided the men up into guards and crew. The crew went about the normal ranch chores, while the guards rode designated areas of patrol, watching out for Bannister.

'Sonuver's likely a hundred miles away, sittin' drinkin' a cold beer or sweet-talkin' his wife into the bedroom, an' here's me only halfway through my patrol.'

And he knew it would be recorded and reported by someone. Damned if he knew just who it was who was spying on the guards and reporting back to Cordell. Likely someone was making a note of him resting and having a smoke now, this very minute.

'Well, good luck, you lousy snoop!' he said half-aloud. 'I find out who you are and you better check your bunk for a rattler, that's for sure.'

'Now that's a real dirty trick, *amigo*,' a voice said softly behind him and Shiloh rolled away from the tree, quick as a snake dodging a mongoose.

His six-gun came blurring up out of leather. Then a shadow crossed his face and he got a brief look at a tall man with something glinting crosswise across his chest. A boot crushed his wrist to the gravelly ground and twisted, causing Shiloh to yell in pain but he didn't feel it for long.

The brass-bound butt of a rifle smashed between his eyes and the world exploded into slivers of bright light that streaked off somewhere, leaving only oblivion.

He didn't know where he was when he came round — head and neck-muscles full of burning, throbbing pain, his hands tied with rawhide drawn tight behind his back. He was lying on his side and didn't at first recognize the country. Then he realized he was on a slope overlooking a rugged part of Broken C, many miles from where he had sat down for a smoke, a long way from the patrol lines and the ranch house.

He hurt all over and something *clunked!* half-a-dozen times in his neck before he turned his head the other way.

Searing fear knotted his belly as he saw the big man sitting on a log, smoking silently, a Henry rifle with a long, octagonal barrel resting on the log beside him.

He swallowed bile, recognizing Steve Bannister.

'Christ! How'd you — you get past the guards?'

'They're all like you, Shiloh, want to rest up, take it easy, instead of doing the job properly. Hell, a band of Chiricahuas could ride through here, and unless they were yodelling their war cries no one would know.'

Shiloh felt an urge to urinate but tried to ignore it. 'I-I'm only doin' what the boss told me. I'm just a cowhand most of the time.'

'Cowhand and trouble-shooter,' Bannister corrected calmly. 'I know about you, Shiloh. You beat-up on a man I worked for once, hadn't seen me in years, but you still crippled Ed Ryler — place called Plum Mountain, Tennessee.'

'Was that his name? Hell, I ain't thought about him in years.' He tried to sound tough, uncaring.

Then he started to writhe and scream as Bannister flicked his half-smoked cigarette into the opening of his shirt below his sweaty, grimy neck.

'Get it off! Get it off! Judas *priest!* Get . . . it . . . offa me!'

Bannister made no move and Shiloh rolled about frantically until the burning, now flattened, cigarette finally spilled out after his struggles had torn two buttons off the shirt so that it popped open. Sweating, gasping, lying on his side, he stared up at Bannister.

'Heard, too, it was you smacked Widow Petersen silly in Pemberton Falls, Colorado. I stopped at her cabin for two days, chopped some wood for her, repaired some shingles, swung a barn door. She fed me well and gave me a full grubsack to take with me. That was seven years ago and I sent her a Christmas card once, from Santa Fe, passin' through with a trail herd. How the hell did you think she'd know where I was two years back when you beat her up?'

By now, Shiloh was starting to see where this was leading. He licked his lips.

'Someone told us you worked for her — never said how long back, nor that it was just for a coupla days.'

'And you didn't stop to find out, just waded in and knocked that old lady into the middle of next week. I heard she never fully recovered, was vague and childish, couldn't even walk without a stick. It was a mercy she died last year.'

Shiloh was feeling that urge to urinate again, having a lot of trouble ignoring it now.

'McQueen must've spent a heap of Cordell's money while he was in Yuma, hunting for me.'

Shiloh nodded readily. 'Yeah! Yeah, he-he wanted Rance to know he was lookin' hard; had notions of mebbe gettin' a partnership in Broken C.'

'He could've just made a token search. Being locked up in Yuma, Cordell would never know different.'

'Like hell!' Shiloh was happy to turn the subject off himself. 'Cordell's got plenty friends in high places an' they weren't just workin' to get him a parole — they were keepin' an eye on McQueen — on all of us. Still are.'

Bannister nodded, not showing his surprise: he hadn't realized Cordell had a whole slew of partners in his many crimes, still working on his behalf in the background. But, naturally, they would be interested in him. Men like that would always be worried by the possibility that Cordell, if not receiving the attention he felt was his due, might turn state's evidence and implicate them all.

'What-what you gonna do with me?'

'Shiloh, I'd like to string you up to this damn tree. Fact is, I'm still deciding. You deserve to die and more than once I thought about leaving Linda and Tess for a spell while I hunted you down. But with snakes like you and McQueen and the rest of the Broken C scum on the loose, I didn't dare leave my family.'

'You . . . you've left 'em now.'

'Because I *know* they're safe which makes you unlucky.'

'Aw, now, wait up! I-I only did what I was told! Judas, man, you work for

Rance Cordell and you do what he tells you an' do it damn *good* or you disappear.'

Bannister lifted the heavy Henry and slammed Shiloh across the shins with the massive octagonal barrel, scraping downwards, ripping off six inches of skin. Shiloh screamed as blood soaked through his trousers.

'Je-sus *Christ*!'

'You're no better'n the maggots in the bottom of an outhouse, Shiloh. You think you'd be missed if I killed you right this minute? Hell, the world'd be a better place! I dunno why the Good Lord lets you and your kind live and walk this earth. You wouldn't even make good fertilizer, you're so rotten.'

Bannister regained control, fighting down the pent-up fury that he had been living with for the past ten years. He forced himself to take several deep breaths and, as he noticeably settled down, Shiloh relaxed some, face still grimacing as waves of agony from his throbbing, skinned shins still plagued him.

Bannister stood above him and Shiloh's dirty face became all blotchy as blood drained from it.

'Decided what I'm gonna do with you, Shiloh. Something for you to think about. You're gonna die.'

'No! No! Judas, don't . . . '

Bannister casually kicked him in the ribs, terminating the man's pleas.

'Oh, I'm not gonna kill you — not directly. I reckon we'll leave that to Cordell. One more murder won't bother his conscience none, and he'll be shook up when he realizes I got through his guard line. And you talked to me . . . you *are* gonna talk, ain't you, Shiloh, old *amigo*? Yeah. Sure you are. Might have to persuade you some, but you'll talk.'

This time, Shiloh was unable to prevent his bladder from voiding.

★ ★ ★

Rance Cordell had just finished supper and was cutting the end off one of his cigars that were specially imported from Cuba for him, when he heard the commotion in the dark yard outside.

Already nervous — and despising himself for it — Rance dropped the cigar cutter and lurched to his feet, listening to all the shouting, the whinnying of a frightened horse, the curses of his men.

The Mexican housekeeper, standing by to see if her boss required coffee, put a hand to her mouth and her eyes widened as she turned and bolted through the door that led back to the kitchen. It was none of her business.

Cordell didn't even notice. His own eyes were focused on the doorway leading to the front entrance hall. He tensed, feeling slightly dizzy, as he heard the front door open and heavy boots hurrying down the passage.

Mace McQueen, sweaty-faced and looking worried as hell, stood there,

188

gulping, before he blurted out, 'He's here! Bannister's here! He's gotten past the guards an' — '

'The hell're you talking about?' demanded the rancher, his heart starting to thump in his chest like an Indian war drum. 'How the hell . . . ? Where is he?'

McQueen stepped inside and jerked a thumb over his shoulder. 'Shiloh's outside.'

'Goddammit, I don't care about Shiloh! *Where the hell is Bannister?*'

'Who knows? He sent Shiloh back, tied him to a rope behind his hoss an' dragged him three or four miles at least. He's in a helluva state.'

'How d'you know he didn't fall and catch his boot in a stirrup?'

''Cause his hands are tied with rawhide and the rope's around his ankles! And, Lordy, you oughta see his shins!'

'How d'you know it was *Bannister*?'

McQueen stepped closer and held out a dirty, crumpled piece of paper.

'That's blood on it as well as dirt. Shiloh's blood.'

Cordell took it between his fingertips, turned it towards the lamp so as to read crudely printed words.

No further use for this Judas.
He's told me all I need to know.
You can have him — maybe I'll
bring the next one in person.

It was unsigned but there was no need for any signature. Rance crumpled the paper into a ball, hurled it wildly in the direction of the stone fireplace.

'*Find* the son of a bitch! If he's close enough to jump Shiloh and send him in draggin' behind his horse, he can't be far away. Get men searching! *Now!*'

McQueen was glad enough to get out of the room and start yelling at the men to get horses and guns: they were going looking for Bannister.

There were no volunteers called for: they had their orders, and every man who rode out knew he better obey or lose his job — at least. One man opted to quit and Cordell told him from the porch steps, 'Then get off my land!'

'I need to draw my pay, Mr Cordell, and — '

'Get . . . off . . . my . . . land! You quit without notice, you don't get paid.'

'Hell's teeth! I'm due almost the full month!'

Cordell leaned on the rail. 'Myers, you can try to collect the dollars you think you're owed, or be certain of collecting a ten-cent bullet if you don't start packin' your warbag right now.'

Myers turned and ran for the bunkhouse.

A dozen riders were milling in the yard now, no one happy at the thought of trying to find Bannister at any time — let alone in the dark.

'That five hundred bounty still on, boss?' an anonymous voice called from deep within the pack.

'Just boosted it to a thousand bucks! Kill him if you have to, but if you can bring him in still breathing, I'll double it.'

In a couple of minutes, the yard was empty except for the clouds of settling dust. Cordell turned to McQueen who was standing at the foot of the steps.

'You sleep in the house tonight, and bring your shotgun. Send someone to find Casey, too, and pick three of the best to guard the house permanent.'

'Gonna be stretchin' the lines pretty thin, Rance. We're shorthanded as it is with so many ridin' line all the time on the lookout for Bannister.'

'Do it!'

McQueen started to move away, gestured to where Shiloh lay huddled and motionless in the dust, the rope still tied around his ankles but the other end released from the saddlehorn.

'What about Shiloh? He's still alive.'

'He better not be when next I see you.'

Cordell hurried back into the house, stomped down to the office and went to the cupboard where he kept his guns.

His hand was shaking, he noticed, as he opened the door lock with its brass key.

★ ★ ★

Although the early grey light was weak, Banister was still able to see the frantic activity on the Broken C.

He was high up on a ridge now, on his way back to his cave. He had been covering his tracks when he figured there was enough light for him to use his field-glasses. There were riders everywhere down there: men patrolling the fence lines with rifles balanced on their knees or just being held in one hand at the ready. Others were literally beating the brush with heavy branches while three or four mounted men sat behind them with guns cocked in case they flushed him.

More men, he noted on a slow, careful sweep of the glasses, had climbed trees or high boulders and were searching with their own glasses and telescopes.

Wherever he saw men, there were guns.

He smiled thinly: so the manhunt was on. He must have shaken up Cordell considerably by sending in Shiloh like that.

Fine with me, Cordell.

He was still a long way from his cave and he slid back from where he had been lying full-length on a projecting rock above the slope, dropped down into the brush where the dark-brown Flecha waited. He had the strange thought that its lean Arab lines made it seem so sleek that it was almost as if it was moving, while standing still.

The sun was two hours in the sky above the sprawling rangeland before he reached his cave. He was outside of Broken C land here but eventually, he knew, they would run their search for him this far out.

So, maybe he should give them a diversion that would keep them busy on the far side of Cordell's land.

While he set up his camouflage across the cave and hobbled Flecha on the best-hidden patch of grass, he took one last long searching look at the distant ranch.

Something glistened over there, a giant-size mirror, sparkling through the trees like falling diamonds. It was a large body of water where he figured only a creek was running, according to the map he was using. None of his information had mentioned a lake in this area . . .

And, of course, it wasn't a lake, but maybe it could be called a man-made version of one.

It was the Broken C dam, their main water supply, that irrigated pasture land through an extensive system of valve-controlled pipes Cordell had laid at great expense, making his spread the most prosperous in the whole south of Arizona. Its nickname, given to it by other, envious ranchers, was *Green Pastures* and Cordell had rubbed it in by frequently quoting an old adage:

'The grass is always greener on t'other side of the fence — *my* fence, anyways!'

Steve Bannister smiled to himself as he spread his blankets back in the shadows of the cave, and lay down, ready for sleep.

He was sure he was going to have pleasant dreams.

13

Linecamp

Yesterday, he had heard two or three dull thuds off to the north. He recognized them as small dynamite explosions, probably ranch hands clearing a few stumps while preparing more pastures for Cordell's herds.

Steve had stayed away from that area in case there was a concentration of cowhands working there.

But now he needed to get close — and do it without being spotted by the many other Broken C hands riding the fences and boundaries, looking for him. If they saw him — what? Shoot on sight? Take him in, dead or alive?

Shiloh had told him Cordell had put a thousand-dollar bounty on his head, but claimed he wasn't sure whether he was wanted dead, or to be brought in with enough life still in him so Cordell could have the pleasure of watching him die, or even deliver the killing shot himself.

Only once before in his life had he had a bounty on him — a long time ago, in Oregon, after he had got caught up in a brawl with some lumberjacks. He was still in his early twenties at the time, not long after he had given evidence that had seen Cordell jailed in Yuma, when he found himself facing the biggest lumberjack he had ever seen. A mad French-Canadian whose wife had run off with another man while he was in the wilderness cutting timber — a young man, in his early twenties.

Crazy with booze and jealousy, the Frenchy had focused all his hatred on Bannister and would have killed him if Steve hadn't been wearing a six-gun at that time.

Known only as 'Kid' because of his age and boyish good looks, Steve shot the man dead. He had been aiming to wound but, hands shaking from fighting, the gun had wavered and the bullet had taken the Frenchy through the heart. The lumberjacks — and other uninvolved drinkers — said it sure looked to them like the Kid had fired with the intention of killing the big man.

Still holding the smoking pistol, the angry 'jacks closing in, he fired twice more, wounding two more men. Then, in the confusion, he had got away via the rear door.

A week later, riding through a strange town, he saw a crude likeness of himself on a wanted dodger nailed to a post outside a general store: he was wanted for murder and wounding in a backwater town called Rollinglog. And there was a $500 bounty on his head.

He had immediately gone south, but there had been two attempts to collect the bounty, so he turned east, then south again, and, finally west, letting his hair grow and a smudge on his jowls that was an embryo beard. He had put his six-gun away in the bottom of his saddle-bags, deciding it could not be trusted in his hands: it could not be aimed as accurately as a rifle, because a revolver could not be held as steady.

For all he knew that bounty still stood; he remembered how he had hated the feeling that he was now no more than just a high-priced piece of meat.

But that was long ago. Cordell's bounty didn't bother him. He knew the Broken C hands would be trying hard to earn it, but he figured he could keep clear of them.

By devious trails, once swimming the brown horse upstream in a deep part of the boundary river, he drew closer to where the men were working clearing the land. He could hear the double-handed saws and axes felling the trees, so maybe they would be blasting today, or early tomorrow.

He came on to a break in the timber and found he was on a small hogback rise that sloped gently down to where three men were felling tall trees. Halting the horse and leaning forward in the saddle so he could peer between low branches, he checked thoroughly: yes, only three men. Two felling, the third trimming.

As he watched, the trimmer thunked his axeblade into the felled tree he was working on and wiped sweat from his face, pressed big hands into his aching back.

'Take a break. I'll go fetch the dynamite and blast them stumps. We can work it so it'll take us through to sundown, give us an easy afternoon.'

'Best not risk it, Cass,' one of the tree-fellers said. 'Boss ain't in any mood for that kinda thing.'

'Listen, I've had a helluva lot of ridin' lately, down to the ferry and so on, late nights guardin' the boss. I'm gonna take it easy — and to hell with you two — just keep quiet about it or you know what'll happen. I'm doin' more'n my share and I've had a bellyful. *An'* my wound's achin'.'

'Judas, Cass, you get paid extra, bein' one of Rance's protectors — and you're the explosives expert, so you'll get extra for that, too! I don't see what you got to bitch about.'

Cass Taylor narrowed his eyes. 'You shut your mouth, Frost! And you, too, Pork, before you start.' The men stood there awkwardly, obviously afraid of this man. 'I'm goin' now and I'll take my time gettin' back. Leave just enough daylight to blast. Might even leave it all till tomorrow.'

The tree-fellers looked dubious but Cass, heavy-shouldered, though not very tall, was already walking towards three horses tethered in the shade. One foot in the stirrup, he looked contemptuously at the axemen.

'Pair of choirboys! You let Cordell buffalo you. Hell, he's only a man.'

'The man who pays the wages.'

'You should see some of the hell-busters I've worked for. You let 'em kick you around, more they'll do it. Tell you what: you boys fill in the rest of the afternoon howsomever you want, I'm goin' back to camp and brew up some coffee, mebbe fry a little sowbelly, an' then I'm gonna take a nap!' He flexed his big shoulders. 'I'm stiff and sore trimmin' these damn trees. Don't matter to me if we don't blow 'em till tomorrow. An' when you come in at sundown, if I'm still sleepin', don't bother to wake me!'

Drop-jawed, they watched him ride on out.

'He's loco!'

'I wouldn't tell him that! He's a damn killer. Him an' his sidekick, Casey — Cordell's killers. They don't take no crap from anyone.'

Pork lifted his axe and started a swing towards the deep V they had started in the tree.

'Well, I know *I* ain't tough enough to go agin Cass Taylor or Cordell. I'm just gonna do the job I'm s'posed to.'

As the axe thudded home, the second man shrugged and said, 'Best thing, I reckon. Gimme some room . . .'

The tree crashed to the ground with a thundering noise behind Bannister, just as he topped-out on the crest of the hogback and dropped over to the far side.

Below, following a narrow trail along the creek, was Cass Taylor, riding at his own pace, whistling. *Cocky, uncaring — maybe some of it was bravado, seeing as he was out of Cordell's sight. But to Bannister, Cass Taylor was living out his last hours. He just didn't know it yet.*

Shiloh had told him it was Cass Taylor who had backshot Jack Tatum: it wasn't true, but it had to've been Cass or Chico. Neither were friends of Shiloh's.

Now, Bannister could see part of a small lineshack up ahead, screened by trees. He turned the brown upslope, allowing it to make its own way. He could see a trail that would allow him to approach that shack from the rear.

He smelled frying bacon as he made his way down on foot, towards the linecamp. The sun was heeling over and visibly sinking towards the ranges now. Rifle in one hand, the other grabbing at bushes and saplings so he didn't stumble, Bannister closed in. The smell of the cooking was making him salivate: Taylor, preparing his snack before settling in for his late afternoon nap.

The big man was sitting on an upturned box in front of a blackened fireplace at the back of the long single-roomed lineshack, the skillet sizzling and sputtering. It kept him from hearing Bannister's light footstep as he came in the open door.

'Smells good, Cass, I been eating hardtack for the past couple of days.'

Taylor heaved himself backwards off the box, bringing the skillet with him and tossing its contents over his broad shoulders. The grease and bacon strips and a ladleful of beans shot towards Bannister as he lifted his rifle. He instinctively ducked and slipped to one side but some of the spraying hot grease stung his left cheek and the side of his neck. He went down with a clatter, crashing into a roughly made pine table, overturning it.

Then Cass Taylor was on him. The man didn't bother with a gun, although he was wearing a Colt. He flung his heavy body on to Bannister who was floundering on hands and knees, knocking him flat to the floor. Steve lost his grip on the Henry and it skidded away into the overturned table. Cass drove a meaty fist into Bannister's midriff, smashing the breath from him, his legs rising involuntarily.

The Broken C man rose to his knees and both fists sledged into Bannister, one connecting with the side of his jaw. Steve rolled, senses spinning. Taylor came hurtling after him and slammed full-force into a raised boot. It took him on the thick neck, spun him to one side with a choking grunt.

He was tough. Normally, such a kick would have put any average man down for the count. He was slowed, but rolled completely over and thrust to his feet, beating the rising Bannister by a split second. It was enough for him to swing a fist like a leg of venison. Bannister managed to stop his forward movement in time, but the knuckles smashed into his shoulder, still with enough force to spin him sideways into the wall.

Cass scooped up the hot skillet that had fallen to the floor and swung at Bannister's head. It whistled past, clanged against the wall and jarred from Taylor's grip. Crouched, Bannister drove himself forward with a roar, arms working as he pummelled the thick, muscle-padded midriff. Cass yelled as his shotgun wound was hit. Steve rammed his shoulder into the man, wrapped his arms about him and, legs driving, rammed forward again. The motion carried them through the doorway and out on to the gravel and coarse grass. They rolled and kneed and punched when they had room, coming up short against the single step up into the shack. Bannister's head struck the hardwood slab and a cascade of fireworks burst behind his eyes. Cass hit the small stones propping up the step with his jaw and he thrust away, bloody-mouthed.

Bannister, on his side, groggy, lashed out with a leg. The boot took the other on the neck, spilling him downslope. Cass scooped up an apple-sized rock and flung it at Steve who floundered halfway across the stoop, upper body in the shack proper. The rock shattered on the doorpost, raking his face like shrapnel.

He clawed at his eyes and, through clutching fingers, saw Taylor was on his feet, reaching for his Colt.

Steve did a backward somersault that took him all the way into the shack. Cass's lead sliced a humming splinter from the doorway as the man lunged forward in a staggering run, smoking gun barrel trying to line up on Bannister.

Steve dived for his rifle, got a hand on the stock as the Colt fired again. He winced as lead burned a short line across one cheek and then he was on his back, levering and triggering as Cass's wide body filled the doorway, Colt still blazing.

The rifle bullets took Taylor just under his throat and he was brought up short as if someone had yanked a rope tied about his thick waist. His head jerked on his thick neck. His mouth sagged open and blood spilled over his jaw as tree-trunk legs began to fold. He was dead where he stood, but gamely tried to lift his six-gun for one more shot. Bannister lifted the rifle, but didn't need to fire.

Cass Taylor crashed against the wall hard enough to make the shack tremble, spun off and landed on his back. The whites of his eyes showed briefly before they closed forever.

Steve dragged him inside and dropped him beside the front wall to one side of the doorway, out of sight of anyone approaching the camp.

Stumbling, he righted an overturned chair and dropped into it, body throbbing. He sat there, recovering his breath, then reached up to his cross-chest bullet belt and thumbed two cartridges from the loops. He slid them into the Henry's magazine.

The sun was drawing long, heavy shadows across the linecamp now. He sat with his rifle in his lap. This was a long way from the place where the trees were being felled, and there was a hogback in between. He didn't think the shooting would have been heard by the other tree fellers.

His ears were still ringing as he waited for them, but it was almost full dark before they came riding slowly up to the shack.

They were mighty tired, dozing in their saddles. The horses knew the way and stopped when they were within a couple of yards of the cabin. The cessation of movement brought both men awake, blinking.

One slurred, 'That damn Cass! Must be still asleep, the lazy fool.'

'Likely sleepin',' agreed the other

man with some bitterness. 'Not even a lamp. Ah! There he is in the doorway now.'

'That ain't Cass!' the first man almost shouted.

They froze as Bannister worked the rifle lever.

'Just step down easy, boys, don't want to harm you. Shuck your guns, then one of you can cook us something to eat while the other shows me where Cass keeps his dynamite. Now, that's fair, ain't it?'

They didn't say whether they thought it was fair or not, but they obeyed. Pork did the cooking while Frost showed Bannister where the dynamite was stored, under a trapdoor in the floor, in a stone-lined pit. Steve whistled: there was enough there to blow up the whole damn shack if he wanted to.

'All right, Frost, get that box up here and be careful with the detonators and fuses.'

Frost clambered down into the pit reluctantly.

It was a poorly cooked meal but filling and the coffee was hot and strong. Pork and Frost stayed on one side of the shack while Bannister sat, smoking, in a rickety chair. He seemed to be studying them and they squirmed uneasily.

'Listen, we ain't part of the manhunt for you,' Frost said, almost hurling the words across the room. 'Cordell's got special men for that; we keep the spread runnin'. It's only once in a while we sort of work together. Like Cass is — was — the explosives man, used to work the mines in the Superstitions. I-I hope you ain't gonna kill us.'

Pork dropped the tin mug of coffee he was lifting towards his fat mouth as Frost spoke. 'Jesus! No!'

Bannister lifted a hand. 'You're safe, boys. You'll be a mite uncomfortable for a spell, but you'll get outa your bonds eventually. I'll leave your horses down amongst the trees.'

When he had finished his smoke he had Pork tie Frost hand and foot, then

212

he inspected the bonds and, satisfisfied, tied up Pork the same way. He gagged them both, carried them out to some boulders, thirty yards from the shack.

Then he opened the explosives box, sorted out a length of the slow-burning fuse. There were old newspapers and tattered copies of *Harper's Weekly* scattered around. He crumpled these and dropped them on the floor. He stacked kindling from the wood box near the fireplace over the papers, smashed a box and two chairs, and stacked this around the pile.

Then he pulled the lead from half-a-dozen cartridges taken from the dead Cass Taylor's bullet belt and poured the powder under the newspapers. He poked the end of the fuse in the powder heap and trailed it out through the door and lit the end. It smouldered, burning very slowly.

He figured between thirty and forty minutes before the spark reached the powder and set it off. Pork and Frost would never get free of their bonds in that time, but they would be safe from the fire.

And, by then, they would have plenty of company with men riding up from the ranch to try to put out the fire that was destroying the linecamp.

And while they were busy doing that, he would set the dynamite and blow Cordell's dam to hell.

14

To the Death

He used way too much dynamite.

It was a long time since he had handled any kind of explosive and he underestimated the power of the modern day dynamite. Working below the leaking headgates in the starlight — and racing against the rise of the moon — Steve tilted his head back and looked up at the dripping wall of logs and earth towering above him.

It was like a miniature mountain. *How many sticks would it take to blow out the gates? Would the collapsing gates bring down the wall above them, or would he need to plant dynamite halfway up?*

All he knew was that he wanted all the dam's millions of gallons of water to flood Broken C. The way the land lay, it would surge down in the hollows below the ranch house and its outbuildings, isolating them. There were men riding nighthawk and guarding the fences, but they ought to have time to get out of the way. If not . . .

Well, all he hoped was if some were caught that Cordell and his hardcases were among them. He had to end this now and if there were casualties other than Cordell then he would just have to live with that.

Abruptly ending speculation, he decided to use all the dynamite he had and to hell with it. If it blasted down half the mountain, too bad.

He unrolled the fuse — not as long as he would have liked! But he primed it swiftly with the detonator, setting it deep within a pre-slit stick in the middle of the bundle. It took several vestas before one flared enough to get the fuse burning. He didn't waste any time clambering away from the gates and racing across the slope to where he had left the brown horse, high above.

Beyond, up on the ridge, he saw the linecamp was burning. At last! He had been getting worried that it wouldn't catch fire before he had the dynamite set at the headgates. From here, he could see the lanterns in the ranch yard as men ran around getting mounts from the corrals, piles of old bags from the barn. No doubt Cordell was shouting his head off, screaming at them to get up there and put out that fire before it set the whole blamed mountain ablaze.

He figured the first of the Broken C men must be almost to the linecamp by now — then the dam blew.

He had badly misjudged the fuse's burning time. By now he should've been over the crest. But he was only halfway there.

The blast literally shook the mountain. The brown horse staggered, legs propping and scrabbling for a secure foothold, whinnying, jerking its head, almost going down.

A gout of flame and debris erupted like a volcano, splintered logs and earth and man-sized rocks shattering, hurtling through the night. Against the stars he saw the tops of trees sliced off. Thousands of leaves swirlied like a dark snowstorm across the flash-lit sky.

Then the blast wave hit and knocked him flat, lifting him clean out of the saddle and dropping him as if he had been pushed off a cliff twenty feet above. The horse fell on its side, kicking and whickering, heaving and convulsing. Finally staggering to its feet, it disappeared over the crest to the other side of the mountain, tail and mane streaming, leaving Steve afoot.

He was deafened by the noise, and the blast hurled stones and twigs like buckshot, bringing involuntary gasps from him as they flayed his body. By some fluke he had managed to hang on to his rifle — but the cross-chest bullet belt was still hanging on the saddlehorn where he had left it when climbing down to the headgates.

His eyes felt as if they had been turned inside out and were stinging with grit. Dazed, senses all a-swirl, he sat down, minus his hat, one shirt sleeve in tatters. He could hear nothing, only a kind of humming vacuum filling his head. His balance was out of kilter, sending him staggering wildly when he tried to walk. He flopped down again, blinking, seeing the surging water disappearing at an alarming rate through a huge gap where the dam wall had once stood. It was mighty strange, seeing all that surging torrent inundating the country below, sweeping everything before it, something that was no less than a tidal wave — and he couldn't hear it.

Once it cleared the narrow space where the river had been dammed, the flood spread over the land, unstoppable, tearing up trees and boulders and fence posts, roaring through pastures and taking bawling, floundering cattle with it — and probably some of the nighthawks, too.

Every time he tried to get to his feet his head felt as if it was about to fall off his shoulders. He flopped back, clawing wildly for support, afraid he was going to fall off the planet.

He vomited, disoriented, his blast-slammed body rebelling, trying to cope with the out-of-balance inner ear. In the end, he passed out, still hearing nothing.

When he awoke, the world was roaring around him, full of screeches and thuds, whines and crunches and grunts. He eased up gingerly, groggy, sat with his head in his hands, afraid to open his eyes. After a while he realized the crazy noises were diminishing. As he put one hand down to steady himself, he knocked his rifle *and he heard it clatter!*

Thank God! He could hear again!

And he could see OK now — the moon had risen while he had been unconscious. His jaw sagged as he saw the huge amount of destruction he had caused. A mighty gash torn in the side of the mountain and, beyond, an inland sea. Even as he watched the waters were draining off in a hundred different directions, into natural gutters and holes and trenches.

There were carcasses of cattle floating around, spinning as the surge took them. A horse or two — and at least one human body. Sagging fences stood above the muddy water, wire trailing, posts splintered.

The whole range was wet and soggy for as far as he could see, grass and brush and trees torn up by the powerful flood. It even reached into the ranch yard, lapping around the barns and bunkhouse. The big house seemed mostly untouched — the windows had blown out on the front and the porch had a crazy tilt. Gesticulating figures appeared, staring at the chaos. Suddenly someone spotted him, pointing and shouting, as he lurched to his feet, using the rifle for support.

By the time he was reasonably steady they were running for the only corral whose fences weren't destroyed. Nervous horses milled and snorted behind the rails.

Damn! They were coming after him! And he was afoot with only his rifle's magazine full of cartridges.

Before he turned and staggered up the rise towards the crest of the mountain, he saw four men hurriedly saddling mounts. They would soon ride him down and he knew he could expect no mercy from Rance Cordell, not after this.

He stumbled away, falling several times.

★   ★   ★

'I want that son of a bitch! Ride him down, shoot his legs out from under him, but *bring him to me still breathing*!'

Cordell could hardly speak for the fury surging inside him. Casey held a big grey gelding while the rancher mounted. McQueen handed him his rifle and turned back towards the house.

'No you don't! Get mounted! You're

not sitting home in comfort while we hunt Bannister down!'

'You going to leave the house unattended with Bannister on the loose?'

'He won't be on the loose for long! Get a horse and a gun! Start earning your keep.'

McQueen flushed: he didn't deserve that, not the way he had worked his butt off while Cordell was in Yuma. The man had no cause to complain: the ranch had prospered and he had contacted the right people, spread the money where it did the most good, and got Cordell his damn parole! Now he was treating him like a roustabout in front of the other men.

Silently fuming, McQueen went into the house, got a hat and a rifle. Outside, the others were already riding off: he had to catch and saddle a mount for himself.

Steve had had hopes that he might find the big brown Flecha waiting on the far side of the crest, but there was no sign of the horse. It had had one hell of a fright with that tremendous explosion and was likely still running.

He was light-headed again, rested against a boulder. Below, his pursuers were skirting the floodwaters, silver explosions about the horses' feet catching the moonlight, giving some idea of their speed.

Flat out! Risking falls and injury to get to him!

Gulping air, he turned and dropped down the steep slope. His feet went out from under him and then he was sliding and half-rolling. As he made a fast but precarious passage down to the hollow below, he grabbed a bush, but it pulled free, wrenching his arm. Desperately, he turned on to his belly, able to dig in the toes of his boots to slow him, and use knees, and one hand — the other had his rifle held in a death grip. He slowed and threw himself to the side. His head banged against a rock or a root, his left arm struck something that numbed it to his shoulder. Branches raked his face, opening the bullet burn on his cheek again.

But the wild slide had stopped, and he lay there panting, head roaring again: he would never hear the horses of the hunters as they closed in! He had to keep moving.

His legs were ready to fold under him as he thrust up and staggered away into the brush. Using his rifle to beat the branches aside, he made some progress, but it was going to be a long night. If he was lucky!

He crashed on, knew the sounds would give him away, but had no choice. The ground started to flatten and he figured he was down in the hollow proper which meant that now he had to climb out!

No! He would stay down here, run along the flatter ground, risking discovery to gain extra speed. The brush was thinner and so were the trees, but he figured there was enough cover for him to make it out to the boulder fields beyond: there would be overhangs and huge rocks there where he could shelter.

He didn't know just what he would find, only that he had to keep ahead of his pursuers for as long as he could force his legs to move.

Pausing in some thicker timber, he leaned one arm against a tree, head hanging, sweat dripping from his hair and jawline and suddenly realized he could not hear the horses. He tried to steady his noisy breathing: he still couldn't hear them. They were no longer shouting to each other. They had to be down on the same level as him by now, unless . . . Hell! Unless they figured he would make for the boulder country and had spread out to cut him off!

They knew the country much better than he did.

He reversed direction. He had no notion of what the country was like that way — his map had left most of it unmarked, which meant unsettled wilderness. This would suit Cordell, because it was the kind of unvisited country close to Broken C that could be used for some of his furtive dealings with renegades and outlaws, even a secret trail across it down to the border.

Right now, it sounded pretty good to Bannister, and he staggered on, wondering how long it would be before his legs and lungs gave out and he collapsed, and they found him that way, helpess . . .

No! He dredged up energy he didn't know he had, and plunged on through thrashing brush, willing the moon to go behind a cloud . . .

Then he fell over an unseen embankment and crashed on to hard ground that slammed his labouring breath from his burning lungs. The back of his head struck something solid and there was an explosion of light that went out quickly — and then, nothing.

He could hear them coming! Sounds penetrated to his dazed brain. He groaned softly as he moved carefully, opening his eyes. It was almost daylight:

the sun was rising and shadows were dappled with patches of greyish-yellow light.

And horses picking their way warily through the brush were clearly audible.

'There's the son of a bitch!'

The voice was hoarse and the words were followed by the crash of a six-gun. It blasted three more times and lead whined off tree trunks as he scrabbled to find his rifle. His hand touched the breech and he dragged it to him, rolled on to his side. Vision was clearing now, though his brain was still sleep-hazed. They were coming in, two along the flat, one on the slope above and to his right.

Instinct driving him, he brought the Henry up and it jarred his shoulder as he triggered. The man on the slope was flung over his horse's rump. Bannister quickly swung the long, octagonal barrel, its very heaviness making it steady for aiming at his next target. He picked off a man shooting a carbine. Lead zipped amongst the tree branches as the man lifted in the stirrups and toppled sideways.

The third rider dropped his six-gun and pawed at his rifle in the scabbard at the same time spurring his mount up the slope. Bannister held his fire just in time: he had to be sure of his target so he didn't waste a bullet.

The horseman urged his mount up the slope, either trying to get away or looking for high ground so he would have the advantage of position. Bannister fired now and the horse slipped and lunged at that moment, stopped the bullet in the head. It folded instantly and the rider crashed into the brush out of sight.

Steve threw himself behind a bush just as one of the other two, wounded but not out of action, got off a shot that spurted dust from a ragged piece of his shirt collar. It startled him and he dropped even flatter, skidded on some loose gravel. Half on his back, he got off two fast shots — cursing himself for wasting lead. But both found their mark

229

and a man jerked upright before tumbling down through the brush.

The one whose horse he had killed, suddenly burst out of the bushes, running, no longer shooting. Bannister was caught by surprise, and by the time the rifle was up to his shoulder, the man had disappeared into the timber.

It was Cordell himself — now on the run, alone since Steve had accounted for two of his hardnosed gunfighters — he thought one was Casey and the other might have been McQueen — they were both out of it now, whoever they were.

His target was ahead of him and had to be killed.

Bannister didn't know where the energy came from but he was on his feet and charging after Cordell now. He saw a riderless horse on the slope and was tempted to try to grab it, but kept going: he was so close to ending it all! He couldn't let Cordell escape now.

They darted upslope and down again through the brush and scattered timber.

Cordell stopped twice and raked the bushes in a frantic attempt to stop Bannister. He must have emptied his rifle, for the second time he tried was with a six-gun.

Bannister crouched when the lead flew his way, stayed put, until Cordell started running again. *There he was!* Steve's Henry came up in a blur and he triggered, levered — and the lever suddenly jammed halfway! Swearing, he knew what had happend and looked at the magazine just to be sure.

It was the Henry's big flaw: a tinplate tube magazine that was prone to dents which blocked the bullet from feeding past it, pushed by the spring which was also weaker than it should be. He had replaced that spring when he had the breech strengthened, but the gun had seen a lot of use since that time. There was a definite dent in the tube, no doubt caused when he had dropped his rifle several times during the chase down the mountain.

But Cordell didn't know that! He

slapped the lever until it was almost closed, the cartridge still jammed, and ran on, holding the rifle at the ready. Cordell fell, twisting, fired again, leapt up and ran. The timberline ended and Steve staggered out on to a ledge above a steep drop into a gulch. He stopped just in time, heard the grunt behind him and turned as the raging rancher hurled himself at him.

Cordell tried to fire but his gun was empty and he flung it at Steve's head. Bannister ducked, came up swinging the rifle. It caught the rancher on one shoulder and he stumbled forward, throwing thick arms around Bannister. The Henry fell and Steve twisted as a knee lifted towards his groin. It skidded off his thigh, rammed into his belly. He gagged and clawed at Cordell for support. The rancher bared his teeth and knocked his hands aside, spat in Steve's face, then stabbed his thumbs at Steve's eyes.

Bannister ducked his head, brought up the heel of his hand under Cordell's jaw. The man's teeth clacked together and his head snapped back. His big body staggered free, and he sagged drunkenly. Bannister drove his knee into that hated face and Cordell rolled down the slope towards the edge of the drop.

Wide-eyed in panic, he managed to stop and twisted aside. Bannister fought to keep from going over the edge with his own impetus. Cordell hurled a rock at him. It caught Steve in the chest and knocked him back from the drop. Cordell spun and lunged away. He yelled as the edge crumbled beneath his weight and dropped from sight. Bannister crawled on hands and knees, saw the man had fallen to a lower ledge and was climbing across and up. He went over without hesitation, dropping recklessly, snatching at jutting rocks: some pulled out of the earth with his weight. But he was oblivious to the danger, focused entirely on Cordell now, a mad lust to kill driving him on.

Cordell glimpsed the face twisted in

savagery and knew what it meant. He made a brief whining sound and started back up to the big ledge. Steve flung himself forward, hand reaching. It brushed Cordell's flapping shirt and the cloth ripped away. Steve floundered, inches away from falling — and by the time he had pulled back to reasonable safety, Cordell was climbing out on to the wider ledge.

Bannister went after him, muscles cracking in his efforts. As his eyes lifted above the broken rim, he saw the rancher waiting for him.

Cordell had picked up Steve's Henry, now swung it up by the barrel, teeth bared in raging triumph as he prepared to bring it down to crush Steve's skull.

Bannister was about to let go and throw himself backwards, taking a wild chance on surviving the fall, when there was a rifle shot.

Cordell jerked, blood splashing at his throat. A second shot punched into his chest and Steve ducked as the man's body toppled over him and plunged down to crumple among the boulders far below.

Blinking, sweat stinging his eyes, Bannister looked up and saw a hand reaching down to help him. He grasped it and was pulled to safety. He sat there and looked up at his rescuer with the smoking rifle in one hand.

'Good to see you again, Ash. Thanks.'

Ash Temple — no badge on his sweat-soaked shirt, Steve noticed — smiled crookedly. 'What're friends for?'

There were riders on the slope, rounding-up some of Cordell's surviving men. A tall young man came striding up the narrow trail. Sunlight glinted from a US marshal's badge on his shirt pocket.

'Trying to steal my thunder, Ash?'

Ash shrugged. 'Meet US Marshal Beau Kimble, Steve.'

As they shook hands, Kimble said, 'Seems you two've closed this case for me.' He gestured briefly to the broken body lying below.

Bannister looked, puzzled.

'We knew Cordell couldn't've got that parole legally. Marshal Parminter ordered an investigation: there had been allegations of graft amongst the judiciary and prisons department for a long time. No one had any proof, but this time we moved in fast enough to identify the men Cordell bribed. Two of 'em sang like canaries to save their own damn hides. We've rounded-up most of the group. I came down here with a half-dozen men to take Cordell back to Yuma where he would've stayed until he rotted.' He shook his head briefly. 'Parminter's a hard man to please, but I reckon he'll be satisfied with this ending. You must be, too, Bannister.'

'Yeah — reckon so. It's been a long time coming.'

'Gonna come back to Babylon, Steve?' Ash Temple asked, but Bannister looked dubious. 'Why not? Linda and Tess are in no danger now. The town'll help you rebuild your business.' Ash gave one of his rare smiles. 'You'll be among friends.'

After a few moments Bannister nodded. 'I've had my bad day in Babylon. It has to be good from here on in.' He grinned wearily. 'Reckon I'll give it a try.'

THE END

We do hope that you have enjoyed reading this large print book.

Did you know that all of our titles are available for purchase?

We publish a wide range of high quality large print books including:
Romances, Mysteries, Classics
General Fiction
Non Fiction and Westerns

Special interest titles available in large print are:
The Little Oxford Dictionary
Music Book, Song Book
Hymn Book, Service Book

Also available from us courtesy of Oxford University Press:
Young Readers' Dictionary
(large print edition)
Young Readers' Thesaurus
(large print edition)

For further information or a free brochure, please contact us at:
Ulverscroft Large Print Books Ltd.,
The Green, Bradgate Road, Anstey,
Leicester, LE7 7FU, England.
Tel: (00 44) **0116 236 4325**
Fax: (00 44) **0116 234 0205**

LAND OF THE LOST

Dean Edwards

Young drifter Hal Harper's welcome to the town of Senora is to look down the barrels of the law — little knowing that the outlaw Tate Talbot and his gang are the elected sheriff and deputies. Talbot, with a wanted poster on his head worth a fortune, decides to collect his own bounty by killing the innocent Harper and claiming the drifter is the outlaw known as Diamond Bob Casey. Harper escapes — but only into the Land of the Lost . . .

THE LEGEND OF TORNADO TESS

Terrell L. Bowers

Author Amy Cole wants more than to write a story — she wants to live one. Her chance comes when she's asked to help to clear a doctor of murder. Amy's investigation takes her to Little Babylon, a bandit stronghold in the wasteland of New Mexico. Meanwhile, Whitney Scott trails a band of killers to Little Babylon and meets Amy. However, working together, Whitney faces an unknown assassin — and Amy's priority, over solving the murder, is to stay alive!

CONFEDERATE PAYDIRT

Robert Anderson

Jim Murphy plays high stakes poker — until he hears about the gold; Billy wants to avoid his old comrade, ex-Union Sergeant, Joshua O'Donnel; Seraphim Angel McCall is just greedy — and nobody trusts anybody. The unlikely four band together, searching for lost Confederate bullion. However, when Zachariah Holmes and his murderous band of Comancheros confront them, in the wastes of the sun-blasted desert, bullets fly. The gold may be there, but will anybody live to retrieve it?